6

Beauty IN THE Fields

The Diary of Ruth's Fellow Harvester

Moab and Israel

About 1200 BC

BakerBooks
Grand Rapids, Michigan 49516

Diary One
Sorrow in Moab

Beside the Arnon River

I'm tucked between two clumps of black irises as my swollen feet dangle in the cool river water. Irises are my favorite flower, and lucky for me, they grow all across Moab. Papa just told me, "You are a flower among flowers, Abi!" He laughed.

Our sheep are slurping the water, paying no mind to my presence. They're used to me by now. I've walked up and down the valley with them since yesterday. Spring is here, so Papa shaved the flocks before we left. Their newly shorn skin is still pink and tender like a baby's. It's important to shear them before the summer sun beats on their backs and they overheat. Besides that, their coats get so bulky that they have difficulty moving around, especially the fat ones.

Papa told me the flocks like to be sung to, so I've made up several songs for them. Sheep don't see very well, but their hearing is excellent, and they'll follow their shepherd's (or in this case, shepherdess's!) voice anywhere. It's been fun, but I'm ready to return home in the morning. I still need to talk to Papa. He doesn't know it, but that's the reason I came with him to graze our flocks in the first place.

Eagles soar above me, searching for prey on the wide plateau to the east. To the west are the sandstone cliffs. I've already spotted two herds of mountain goats climbing over the steep, jagged slopes. On the other side of the cliffs is the Salt Sea. Every year Papa takes Mama and me there to swim. The water is so salty, I can lie on my back and float without even trying. Mama and Papa sit in the water to cure what ails them; the Salt Sea is loaded with minerals, which are said to be healing. These minerals are said to cure skin diseases and aching joints, which Papa has a lot of. There are also pools of hot springs, which bubble up from the ground near the sea. The sulfur in the water stinks, but it's healing too.

My twin brothers don't go with us as often as they used to. They're older now and not as interested. Ahmed and Asher are both fifteen years old. I'm ten.

Papa left me in charge a few minutes ago so he could scout a safe place to spend the night. He returned quickly. "Abi! We have found favor with the gods," he announced. "There's a cave close by. It's a natural sheep pen!"

I smiled at him, but inside I cringed. Last night we slept below the trees in the heart of a small gorge. We were fortunate to stumble upon an old sheep pen built of stones, and I helped Papa repair one of the walls with tree branches. When Papa whistled to the flock, the sheep followed him into the pen. Their bells tinkled around their necks.

He built a fire, and we spread out our cloaks and listened to the river wash over the rocks. I was almost asleep when the hysterical laughter of the hyenas echoed off the canyon walls and froze my blood. I was sure they were creeping closer to us in the dark, circling our camp and jeering at us. The sheep sensed their presence, and feeling the danger around them, they began to prance in the pen, crying out in a chorus of baas. Except for the fire, there was little light. The sky was just a narrow scarf above us, and the moon and the stars didn't give much light. It was a long time before the hyenas were quiet and I could sleep.

The cave is a better choice, but I still dread the thought of sleeping away from home for another night.

First Light

I feel refreshed. Last night as the sun set, we led the flocks into the cave. We slept inside at the mouth of the cavern, and Papa guarded the entrance. Once or twice we heard the howls of the wolves in the cliffs, but mostly it was quiet. It was a perfect time to think.

Since we left home my mind has been busy with thoughts of my friend Ruth. It's a long story, and I should explain it to you like Mama explained it to me. That way you'll know what I'm talking about—you're not just a diary to me, after all; you're my secret friend

Long before I was born, a woman called Naomi

and her husband, Elimelech, were living in Bethlehem in Judah, just west of the Salt Sea. They had two sons called Mahlon and Kilion. There was a great famine in Judah, so Elimelech decided to leave his country and come to Moab, where the food was plentiful and the land was fertile. Papa met Naomi and Elimelech on their crossing to Moab while he was tending the flocks. He liked them right away and helped them get settled near our home in the village of Dibon.

When Elimelech died unexpectedly, Naomi was left alone with her boys. She was crushed. She had left her people and her country, and now she was a widow in a strange land. Mama said she took comfort in her sons and was filled with joy when they married. Kilion took a Moabite woman called Orpah for his bride, and Mahlon chose a beautiful Moabite woman named Ruth.

They weren't together for long before tragedy struck again. Last week Kilion and Mahlon died unexpectedly like their father. Now Ruth and Orpah are widows, and Naomi has no men to care for her. I can't shake the sorrow that hangs over my head like a dark cloak. Orpah is a sweet woman, but she's aloof, and I never grew close to her. Ruth, on the other hand, is like a big sister to me, and Naomi is like a grandmother. I adore them, and my heart cries for them.

I've heard snatches of conversation here and there among the people in the village, and I don't know what to make of it. Just the other day Mama sent me to the fuller's shop to drop off our sheeps' wool for washing and carding. I don't like old Gershom the fuller. In fact, I think he's revolting. He's short and stubby, and his bald head is shiny with perspiration and oil. A thin tuft of wiry hair puffs out from each side of his head, making him look like a bird. He isn't a nice man. He's never liked our family, and he's never treated us well.

Gershom poked through our wool bags. Several of his fingernails were missing, and the ones that remained were yellow and thick. "You know I can't wash the fleece if it's stained with feces," he muttered.

"Yes, Gershom, I know. Papa is always careful to remove every bit of stained wool."

"Is it matted this time?" he barked. "I'm not a miracle worker. If it's matted, why do you bother to bring it to me?"

"It's not matted, Gershom. None of our wool has ever been matted."

He squinted at me with his small, birdlike eyes but didn't comment.

"Any burrs or chaff?"

"None," I replied coolly. I'd decided before I came that I wouldn't allow him to ruffle my feathers.

I was about to walk out the door when he called after me. "It will be ready in seven days."

"Seven days? We always pick up our wool in three days," I said.

"It's a busy time of the year," he spat. "Tell your father I have other customers. I have a responsibility to the villagers of Dibon who are true to their Moabite roots. Those *Israelites* got their due when they came to Moab, and your father will too if he forgets who his gods are. The smoke is rising from the nostrils of Beelphegor. Tell your mother and father *that*."

I was shocked by the evil of his words, and all I could do was stare at him in a stupid way. My skin prickled, and my eyes watered when I turned on my heel and left. The Israelites Gershom referred to could be none other than Naomi and Elimelech and their sons. What a terrible thing to say. Beelphegor is the most important of the Moabite gods, and I don't know what Gershom meant about smoke rising from his nostrils.

I'm still waiting for Papa to return so I can talk to him about these things. At dawn he let the sheep out to graze. I suppose I should venture out from my little niche in the cave, but my bones are lazy this morning. I'm not used to the life of a shepherdess.

Later

Papa was standing near the river, lost in his thoughts, when I went in search of him. I watched him pluck a long blade of grass from the dirt beside him and pinch it between his lips. I knew he would nibble on the sweet, fleshy stem with his front teeth and then carry it in his mouth for a while.

He felt my presence behind him, and he motioned with his hand for me to join him. I tucked myself into the crook of his arm, where I feel safe and secure.

"What's on your mind, love?" he asked me. He pulled the long, dark strands of hair from my mouth and laughed. Papa is quick to laugh, like my brother Asher. "You only chew on your hair when something is on your mind."

We sat by the river and talked for a while.

"I hear people whisper about Naomi and the girls," I told him. "Some people say Elimelech died because he left Israel and came to Moab. Some think her sons died because they married Moabites. I even heard someone say the Moabite god cursed them."

I searched his face as I spoke and tried to read his reaction to my words. Since I'm the youngest of the family, Mama and Papa try to hide things from me. They forget that I'm growing up and I'm not a baby anymore. After all, Mama married

Papa when she was just three years older than I am now.

"Do you think that's true?" I prompted him.

Papa didn't say anything for a long time. "I'm not an Israelite," he said, "and I don't claim to know their God. But I do know the way my friend Elimelech talked about this God of theirs. According to him, he is fair and just. He said there was no law given to their prophet Moses that forbade their association with us. We're all related, after all."

"You mean through Lot?" I asked him. "Lot was Abraham's nephew."

"That's right," Papa agreed. "Lot had a grandson called Moab, and we are his direct descendants. The Moabites and the Israelites are both descendants of Abraham."

Since Mahlon and Kilion died, our neighbors have been more vocal about expressing their displeasure with us. Gershom is the most evil, but there are many like him who feel the same way. Papa said they never liked the fact that we befriended Naomi and Elimelech. They liked us even less when Naomi and Elimelech's sons married our Moabite women. Now they hate us because our women have been made widows.

"But what's wrong with befriending the Israelites if we're all related anyway?" I cried. It's so confusing, and it seems so mean and unfair.

Papa patted my shoulder. "It's complicated, Abi. Part of the Moabites' hostility toward the Israelites is a result of land issues. In days of old, Moab stretched as far north as the mountains of Galaad. The Amorites stole those northern lands from us. Then the Israelite tribes of Reuben and Gad took the lands from the Amorites and settled there. Naturally, we were resentful, and we've battled back and forth ever since."

We sat in silence for a time, and I watched a rabbit munch on the sweet river grasses. Every now and then it froze. Even its sensitive whiskers were motionless.

"What will happen to Naomi and Ruth and Orpah?" I asked. "They have no men to care for them."

"It's too soon to know. We'll visit with them

when we return," he told me. "I suspect Naomi will want to return to her homeland now. There's nothing left for her in Moab anymore. There's no reason to stay."

"And Ruth?" I asked him. "What about Ruth? Can she come to live with us?"

Papa told me we have very little to offer her, but yes, she can live with us. She and Orpah will always be welcome. The bells of the sheep are ringing to us from the fields beyond the river. It's time to move on, time to go home.

Nightfall

Ahmed and Asher returned with the goats just before Papa and I returned with the sheep. Since the goats prefer briar and tougher grasses, and the sheep like the soft, sweet clover, they're grazed apart sometimes.

My brothers are very handsome, and except for a small mole on Asher's left cheek, they look identical! The people in the village get them mixed up all the time. Ahmed is the quiet, sensitive one, and he feels insulted when he's called by his brother's name. Asher, on the other hand, is lighthearted and mischievous and thinks it's funny when people confuse him with Ahmed.

Most of the homes in Dibon have cisterns to collect the rainwater. We're lucky to have two. There's one about twenty paces from our front door that's used for cooking and drinking. We also draw water from it to wash ourselves. We have a larger one in the sheep pen, and that's where I found Ahmed.

The flocks had run into the pen and were pushing one another to get to the water. Ahmed had already watered the goats, and now he was watching the sheep.

"We need a good dog," he muttered. "If we had a good herd dog, my work would be cut in half, and so would Asher's and Papa's."

Ahmed hasn't been himself since Mahlon and Kilion died. He looked up to them like he does Papa, and I can tell he misses them terribly. Asher has been affected too, but it shows in different ways. He disappears more often, and it's harder to pin him down.

I stood beside my brother, and he put his arm around me. (Did I mention that he's affectionate too?) "You need to visit the girls tomorrow," he informed me. "Asher and I walked by their house on our way home. Their door was still open, and fresh water had been dumped out the door again."

This is Naomi's doing. Moabites like Ruth and Orpah don't practice such traditions. Israelites open their doors and leave them ajar when someone dies. They believe this helps the departed soul make its journey upward to their heaven. It also reminds the neighbors that a loved one has passed away. When Elimelech died years ago, Mama said no one understood why Naomi wouldn't close her door during the day. Now the people of the village understand her customs—not that they like them.

Since last week Naomi has been dumping out the water Ruth and Orpah bring in from the cistern. It's another ancient tradition of hers. Naomi told us that in death we are like spilled water. When the water flows from the jars, news of a death flows into the streets and alerts the neighbors. In this case, Naomi is reminding us not to forget her sons. As if we ever could.

I reassured my thoughtful brother that Papa had made plans for us to visit them tomorrow. "Where's Asher?" I asked him.

Ahmed pointed toward the house. A ribbon of smoke rose through the roof from the cooking hearth, and the breeze carried the aroma toward us. I could almost taste Mama's stewed lamb! Asher always shows up for meals, and he's the first to sit and hold out his plate. No matter how sad he might be, he never loses his appetite.

That was late this afternoon. Now it's nightfall, and we're all settled in our house. I'm sitting on the roof, where the moon shines bright on my paper. A few moments ago I was startled by a dog's soft whimper. I peeked over the railing Papa built to keep us from tumbling off, but I saw nothing.

It's common for wild dogs to run through the streets in loyal packs. They howl and they bark, but I've never heard one whimper. They're an annoyance to the villagers because they create such a fuss at night. Several times a week I'm awakened by the howl of the pack. Chaos follows every time—One of the neighbors goes outside and yells at the dogs, then another neighbor yells to the first neighbor and asks him to please be quiet, and on it goes.

If all of that yelling doesn't scare the dogs away, someone throws a rock at them. I usually hear the thud as it lands in the dirt, and then I listen to the scampering of paws as the pack runs away snarling. Tonight there was just a lone whimper. I wonder if one of the dogs is hurt.

A New Day

I wish the sky would open up and dump rain on Moab so all the sadness would wash away like dirt. It will rain soon, since spring has arrived, but Mother said no amount of water can cleanse our hearts of the pain of lost loved ones.

We spent most of the day at Naomi's house.

Papa left Asher and Ahmed at home to tend the flocks. Mama carried a big pot of stewed lamb (she prepared a double portion last night), and Papa and I took the bread and the goats' milk pudding she stuffed into our arms.

Ahmed was right. The door of Naomi's small stone house was open, and the soil outside was muddy. Ruth and Orpah had moved into Naomi's home when their husbands died. Mama called to the women and announced our arrival as we walked through the entryway into a small, open courtyard.

Except for the fact that the house is smaller, it's just like ours. In the open-air courtyard, there are stone hand mills used to grind wheat and barley into flour, a small silo to store the grain, and a mud brick oven to cook in. The small rooms that lead from the courtyard are roofed and are separated by pillars. Timber beams are laid across the upper walls of the rooms to form the roof.

Ruth rushed forward when she saw us. She greeted Mama and Papa cordially, as always, but to me she offered the warmest welcome. She wrapped her arms around me, and she held me so close that I could feel her heart thumping in her chest.

She held me away for a moment. "I called on you the other day, but your mother said you were tending sheep with your father." There was a twinkle in her eye. "So now my Abi is to be a shepherdess?"

I felt my cheeks warm with a blush. "No, Ruth," I whispered to her. "I like the sheep, but it's my brothers, Ahmed and Asher, who will follow in my father's footsteps, not me."

Orpah smiled at us, but she stayed put on a mat spread on the floor. She was dressed, like Ruth, in a long, black mourning tunic. Their dark hair, usually worn loose, was covered with a black veil. Naomi wore a tunic of coarse sackcloth, and she had torn it to express her sorrow. Her hair, which was normally covered with a shawl, hung free on her shoulders.

She held out her hands and kissed each of us on the cheek. She didn't resemble the Naomi I've known for years. Her cheeks were hollow, her eyes were vacant, and her smile was forced. There was also an edge to her voice I'd never heard before.

Ruth's sadness, on the other hand, hadn't changed her beauty. Her eyes are so large; the tears that unexpectedly wet them make them shine like drops of dew. Mama told me later that Ruth has one advantage over Naomi, and that's her youth.

When the day wore on, we sat on a mat and passed around the lamb. We scooped it up with pieces of bread and washed it down with goats' milk. Afterward, we ate the pudding and listened to stories of happier times when Elimelech and the boys were still alive. I watched as sparks were lit anew in the women's eyes. Ruth didn't venture far from Naomi's side all day. Several times I watched her cover Naomi's hand with her own and squeeze it tightly. I longed to pull my friend aside and talk to her like in the old days, but it wasn't the right time.

As we walked home, I felt happy that our company and conversation had cheered the women.

Naomi allowed us to close the door when we left, and I peeked at them one last time as I swung the heavy wooden door on its post. Ruth was draping a cloak over Naomi's shoulders. I didn't see Orpah anywhere.

I asked Papa why he hadn't asked them about their plans, but he said we shouldn't press them. They need plenty of time and space to grieve. No decisions should ever be made when someone is distraught.

"I'll make a prediction," Mama said. We had walked enough paces from the house that Naomi and the girls couldn't hear her words. "Ruth won't leave Naomi. It was apparent today that she dotes on that woman. I've never seen such devotion, not even between a mother and her own daughter."

Papa shrugged his shoulders. "This is quite a devotion you speak of, my wife. Is it so strong that it will cause Ruth to leave her homeland and her gods for her dead husband's mother?"

Mama lifted her eyebrows in a knowing way but said nothing.

"Time will tell soon enough," Papa concluded.

A Trail of Blood

Last evening I heard it again—the soft whimper of a dog. I wasn't the only one this time. Asher was sitting with me on the roof, and he quickly climbed down the ladder. He walked around the whole house and whistled softly.

"No dog," he said when he returned, "but I did find this." He held up a leaf smeared with fresh blood.

"There is a dog somewhere," I cried. "Asher, he's hurt and afraid. He must be hiding."

My mischievous brother has a tender side, and he promised to help me look tomorrow if I agreed to get up with him. He rises earlier than I do because he works in the fields with Papa and Ahmed, but I don't care. If there's a hurt animal out there, I'm going to find it.

Midmorning

Asher woke me before sunrise by waving a piece of hot bread beneath my nose. When I opened my eyes, he grinned at me before stuffing the folded square into his mouth. I'm not hungry or friendly when I first wake up, but he never can remember that. Or maybe he does remember and he just likes to tease me. I growled and pushed him away, and he laughed at me, which annoyed me even more.

He and Papa are not only hungry but also very talkative in the morning. They wake up ready to discuss the news of the world that's carried to us by the merchants. I overheard Papa telling Asher that several trade caravans were expected in the next day or two. The king's highway runs right through Dibon, and once every week or two, a long river of camels bulging with exotic goods stops in our village. It's very exciting.

I watched Papa's eyes stare into space, and I knew what he was thinking at that moment. His question to me confirmed it. "Abi, where's the wool you picked up from the fuller's shop?"

I opened my mouth to explain, but Mama cleared her throat. It was a signal that I should keep my mouth shut and let her explain. "It won't be ready until tomorrow," she told him.

I watched my father narrow his eyes, and I looked away. He's a handsome man, like my brothers, but he can look fearsome when he's angry. I'd meant to tell him what Gershom said when we were at the river, but I forgot.

"That's seven days," he said. "We always pick up our wool in three days."

Mama nodded. "Well, it seems that some of our neighbors aren't fond of us. The ones who never liked us now hate us. The ones who tolerated us are less tolerant. I imagine it will get worse for us now."

Mama handed Ahmed a roll of bread stuffed with curds, and he waved it away. "My own mother confuses me for my brother," he groaned.

"I'm not confusing you with anyone, Ahmed, son of Tarek," she announced tartly. "You can't go into the fields on an empty stomach. Old Gershom the wolf might mistake you for a skinny goat and eat you."

Asher began to laugh at Mama's joke, but he

quickly sobered when Papa glared at him. "Come on, Abi. Let's go outside for a bit. Papa, I'll join you and Ahmed in the fields in a short while."

We started our search for the wounded dog at the place where Asher had found the bloody leaf. I was surprised that it was just beyond our courtyard. We found a trail of blood leading from that spot. Some of it was still fresh and wet, and that meant the dog had returned to his other hiding spot when the sun rose an hour ago.

The plains of Moab are plain and stark, and there aren't many trees. I couldn't imagine where a dog could hide, until we came upon the crumbling altar to Beelphegor. I found this place for the first time when I was six years old. I remember running my hand across the dark splatterings that covered the smooth stones on top. I didn't know at the time that it was old, dried blood I touched. I remember the small bones that poked out of the dirt near the side of the altar. Ahmed was with me at the time, and he looked them over before reburying them. He said wild animals had dug them up, and he wouldn't talk to me about it any more.

Later I heard him talking to Papa about the bones. My brother said they belonged to a small child, and Papa told him that sometimes our people sacrificed children as well as animals to Beelphegor. I covered my ears, and I cried. I'd never returned to the altar until the trail of blood led us there today.

The stones of one side had caved in, and as we approached I heard a low, deep-throated growl. We found the dog cowering among the fallen rocks. He stared at us with piercing black eyes. I was used to the mangy, skinny appearance of the wild dogs and didn't expect such a wiry beauty with a glossy, mottled coat. I hoped his instincts would tell him that we had come to rescue him. Instead, he was wary and afraid, and my brother reminded me that a wounded animal can be dangerous. He cautioned me to stay back, and he approached the animal with slow, careful steps.

Asher pulled a pocket of bread and curds from his tunic and tore off a small piece. He held it toward the dog, and I watched the animal's nose quiver. When Asher tossed it to him, his head shot forward and snatched it up, swallowing it in one gulp.

"He's a bedouin dog," my brother told me. "They use them to herd the flocks and guard the camp. They're smart and very loyal. By the looks of it, he got into a fight with a wolf or maybe a hyena while he was protecting the herd."

"Where's his family?" I asked. I climbed onto the altar, though I was sure Papa would consider it an act of irreverence, and placed the side of my hand on my forehead to shield my eyes from the afternoon glare. I saw none of the black bedouin tents nearby.

"They've moved on by now," Asher said. "Either they couldn't find him or they couldn't wait." He threw out two more pieces of bread, and then he held one in his hand and inched closer. His voice was soft and sweet. It was a tone I've never heard my brother use before. Now the dog eagerly took the bread and cheese from Asher's hand each time it was offered.

My brother reached into his pocket, pulled out another piece, and gave it to me. I repeated the ritual, and by the time I fed the dog the last crumb from my fingers, he was licking my hand. We were friends now.

The dog allowed Asher to carry him back to the house, where he laid him in the courtyard. I was certain Mama would be angry, but she wasn't. She checked him over with her experienced hands and discovered that his wounds weren't deep. They were confined to his right hind leg.

"She needs plenty of rest, not to mention food and water, and she'll be fine," she told us. "You did a good thing today by saving this poor animal. I'm proud of you."

"What will we do with her when she gets well?" I asked. I held my breath and waited for her reply.

"If she stays with us by her own will, then she's adopted us. In that case, we'll welcome her into our home," Mama replied. As she left, she called over her shoulder. "If Papa agrees, of course."

Asher left for the fields, and I've been sitting

with my new friend in the courtyard for the past
few hours. I can't wait until Ahmed sees her. Just
yesterday he talked about how much he wanted a
herd dog. I can't wait to see his expression when
he sees her. Oh, and yes, she's a girl!

A Name for My Friend

I discovered that Mama has a soft place in her heart
for animals. I never knew that before. She was
even the one who suggested a name for the dog.
Every time I got up to leave my new friend, she
whimpered. When I returned to her, she nudged
my fingers with her soft nose until I rubbed her
head. She thanked me by licking me with her wet
tongue. I never knew a dog could be so sweet.

"I think we should call her Zibudah," Mama
said, "because she's been a gift to you."

I've decided to call her Zibby for short. I didn't
tell Mama so, but it suits her better than Zibudah.
Besides, it rolls off my tongue easier and sounds
sweeter to my ears.

We had to clean Zibby's wounds with salt

water to help them heal. I know it must have stung terribly, because she howled and struggled to get to her feet. Afterward, I helped dress her wounds with cloth, tied the strips, and tucked them underneath so she couldn't chew them off. It's my job now to change her bandages twice a day and apply olive oil.

Papa and the boys returned late yesterday afternoon. Asher hadn't told Papa and Ahmed about Zibby, so when Papa walked into the courtyard, he did a double take. I don't think he believed his eyes. "Where's your mama?" was all he said. I didn't even have a chance to answer him before he turned on his heel.

Asher stood in the corner with his hands on his hips and a grin on his face. He watched Ahmed approach me slowly.

"Where did this dog come from?" Ahmed asked.

"Asher and I found her yesterday before you went into the fields," I told him. Ahmed held out his hand, and Zibby sniffed it before she allowed him to pet her. "Mama said her wounds aren't serious. They'll heal in good time."

"It's a herd dog," Ahmed said. "I can't believe you found a herd dog. Did Mama say we could keep her?"

"She said we could as long as Papa agreed," I replied.

Asher laughed from the corner. "Do you really think Papa will have a chance to say no? When Mama makes up her mind about something, that's the end of it."

My brother is right, of course. I don't know what Papa said to Mama or what Mama said to Papa, but nothing else was said to us about Zibby. Asher and Ahmed and I take that to mean she belongs to us now.

The Fuller's Shop Again

I walked to the fuller's shop with a knot in my stomach, but I arrived to find that Gershom was in the back and his wife was tending to the customers in the front. I heard the buzz of voices and laughter before I walked in, but when they saw me they grew quiet. I am, after all, a friend to the Israelites. That makes me a leper to some of the people in our village.

I recognized several of the women, but they acted like they didn't know me. Gershom's wife isn't openly evil like her husband, but neither is she friendly. She nodded in my direction to acknowledge my presence, and then she ignored me for what seemed like a long time. I watched the men in the back and tried to be patient for as long as I could.

There's a large wooden tub in the back room, and old Gershom was bent over it. I was in luck. His back faced the front of the shop, and he didn't see me. Sometimes the loose wool is cleaned first, and sometimes it isn't cleaned until it's been spun into thread and woven into cloth. I couldn't tell from where I stood which form Gershom was washing.

If Mama intends to make cloth from the wool, she has it cleaned and fulled afterward. (By the way, dearest diary, "fulling" means shrinking and thickening the cloth by moistening and heating it.) If Papa intends to trade the wool to the merchants who come through town, he has it cleaned first so he can sell it in a loose bundle. The cleaner and the whiter the wool, the more valuable it is. No one wants sheeps' wool that hasn't been washed well; it's greasy and hard to work with.

The shop is long but narrow. I could smell the strong odor of plant and wood ashes that are mixed with urine and added to the tubs of hot water. This mixture not only cleans the wool and removes the oils but also helps whiten it. I saw what Gershom was cleaning when he held up the piece of cloth and examined it in the light. He dunked it back into the tub and rubbed it against a washboard made of blunt nails. When he was through, he transferred the cloth to another tub for a rinsing before wringing it out and hanging it up to dry.

Another man sat across from him. He held a piece of loose wool in his lap and carded it with a metal brush to untangle the fibers and smooth them in one direction. This prepared the wool to be spun into thread.

I heard Gershom's wife clear her throat and turned to see the other women leave the shop. None of them looked at me. She handed me our wool bags without saying a word, and I likewise handed her a small pouch with several pieces of silver inside. With that, she turned and walked to the back of the shop. I stared at her back for a moment, and then I walked out the door.

On my walk home I decided that I like Gershom's wife even less than I like him. Although Gershom is nasty, at least he thinks I'm worthwhile enough to speak to.

Later

Papa pulled out the wool to inspect it when I returned, but he wasn't happy. He said Gershom had done a passable job but not a quality one. "He's sending us a message," he said. The corners of his mouth were turned down, and his brows were drawn together.

"Perhaps we should return the wool to him and demand that he wash it again. It doesn't even look like it's been carded well," Mother complained.

"No," Papa said. "We'll let the matter rest, but I won't return to him."

"Tarek," Mama said, "he's the only fuller in town. Would you have that I wash all of the wool myself, in addition to the spinning and the weaving and the churning of the butter and—"

My father silenced her with his hand. "We won't return."

Mama sighed in an exaggerated fashion as she looked away.

Word has spread through Dibon that the merchant caravans were spotted on the king's highway just south of Moab yesterday. Papa said they should arrive in the village in the next day or two, and then we can take our wool and trade. We will stop by Naomi's house on the way and see if she and Ruth and Orpah would like to come with us.

Zibby Is Healing

I'm already attached to my new friend Zibby, and she to me! She tries to follow me everywhere even though she walks with a painful limp, but that just endears her to me even more. I've changed her bandages each day, and I can see that her wounds are less tender and swollen. Mama spoiled her last night with several chunks of juicy mutton. She set it aside for her when she prepared our supper. Zibby is a charming beggar. She sits and stares with her large, sweet eyes until Mama gives in.

I went outside this morning to draw water from the cistern, and Zibby followed faithfully at my heel. She spotted the herds in the field, and her ears sat erect on her head. We were standing downwind from the flocks, and her nose twitched and quivered in the breeze. She pawed at the dirt and whined and panted until saliva dripped from her mouth. It's apparent that Ahmed will have his herd dog the instant Zibby's leg heals.

The Merchant Caravans ~ The Next Day

Naomi's door was shut when I came by, and the dirt outside her house was dry. I thought at the time that it was a good omen, a sign from the gods that she and Ruth and Orpah had begun to mend their hearts. I was wrong.

I knocked on the door and waited for several minutes. When it swung open, Ruth appeared with red eyes and tear-streaked cheeks.

"Ruth!" I stammered. "What's happened?"

She drew me into her arms in her warm way, but this time I think she was drawing warmth and comfort from me. "We'll go outside," she whispered and turned to glance behind her. "Naomi is resting." She clutched my arm beneath hers and gripped my hand as we walked.

"Has something else happened?" I asked.

She glanced at me with a small, sad smile. "No," she reassured me. "I'm just worried about Naomi. She suffers so. It's a tragedy to lose a husband, Abi. I know because I've just lost mine. But it's unspeakable to lose a child. She's lost not one but both of her children."

I didn't know what to say. I haven't known what to say since Mahlon died. The whole thing has made me feel small. What do I know about losing a husband or a child?

"Can you imagine how your mother would feel if she lost you and your brothers?" Ruth asked. Her voice was soft and gentle.

I was surprised by her question, and tears stung my eyes. I wiped them away quickly with the back of my hand, and I shook my head and stared at my feet. "I know she would be so sad," was all I could think of to say.

"And if she lost your father as well?"

I tried to picture my mother standing in the courtyard, firing the bread that only she would eat. She would be all alone. Poor Naomi. Now I understand why Ruth worries about her so.

I felt silly asking her if she wanted to come with us to the merchant caravans. It didn't seem like the best time. "Papa thought it would be good for you to get out of the house," I tried to explain.

Ruth brightened, which made me glad I'd asked. We made arrangements for her to meet us on the king's highway where the caravans stop at the edge of town.

Later

Zibby whined pitifully as Papa and I walked away, but Ahmed held her back and stroked her thick fur. "Soon you'll be well enough to run with the herds. Be patient for a bit longer, my friend," I heard him whisper.

Ruth was waiting for us beside a long string of bulky camels. They had just arrived from Egypt, and the merchants were unloading some of the goods. They would trade a little in Dibon while they rested and watered the animals before they continued their journey north to Damascus. None of the people in our village could afford the gold and copper the merchants carried, but we could barter for practical items like papyrus sheets or grain and, occasionally, luxury items like linen.

Ruth was still wearing a long black robe, but this one was embroidered with colorful threads on the sleeves and the hems. It was a traditional Moabite dress. Her long black hair hung to the middle of her back beneath her mourning veil, but her eyes sparkled for the first time in many months. It wasn't surprising that she drew the attention of an Egyptian merchant who held out a sack to her.

I had already lost Papa in the crowd, and I moved beside Ruth so I could peer into the sack. There were yellow, red, blue, and green glass beads. As they caught the sun, they reflected the light, making them sparkle.

"Abi! Aren't they exquisite?" Ruth cried. "I can just imagine an Egyptian princess wearing a necklace made with glass baubles just like these."

I watched the merchant's eyes follow her. His skin was very dark, and it was creased like a dried date. He took Ruth's hand and poured some beads in it, one of each color. Then he pressed her fingers around the beads, closed the sack, and waved her away.

Ruth stared at him, confused. "Oh, no!" she called out. " I can't afford these. I have no money to give you and nothing to barter."

Still the merchant waved her away, and Ruth held out the beads to him. "You don't understand," she tried to explain. "I was just admiring your glass. I'm not in a position to trade for them." He was moving away, and Ruth began to follow him.

"My father wants you to have them," a man said from behind us. He was a younger version of the old merchant. His face was kind, and his eyes were gentle. "He recognizes great beauty when he sees it, and he is expressing his admiration for you. He does not speak your language."

Ruth gazed at him with her wide, dark eyes, and I could see the admiration in the younger man's face as well. "I cannot accept such generosity," she told him.

"Then you will insult my father," the young man replied. "He expects nothing in return."

Ruth looked away for a moment, then smiled and tucked the beads inside her basket. "I do not wish to offend your father, so I will accept your gift. Please thank him for me." She reached for my hand and pulled me along.

"These merchants are very bold," she told me. "Promise me you won't come here by yourself."

I gave her my word. When I looked over my shoulder, I saw the young man smiling.

I looked for Papa as we stepped over piles of dung, but I still couldn't spot him. The noise was deafening, and my head was beginning to ache. The singsong of bartering voices, the bellow of the camels, the occasional argument of disgruntled merchants or customers, and the cries of tired, hungry children—it all rang in my ears like a muffled roar.

A smaller caravan of ten camels was watering at the cisterns. I knew it was from Arabia because the scent of spices and perfumes hung in the air like rain. One merchant held a small yellowish-brown pearl up to the blue sky.

"Look! It is the finest frankincense in the world. See how the sunlight streams through it? The clearer the resin, the more valuable it is! Rich men would kill for this." He laughed at an old woman who stared at it and touched it greedily with her knobby fingers.

Frankincense is valuable like gold, and it's sought after just as much. It belongs in the royal courts of Egypt to the south and Persia to the east, but it can also be found in the temples of Baal and Beelphegor. It's harvested from the trees in Arabia, then packed on camels to begin its journey over many long and difficult roads. It's traded numerous times from one caravan to another. The traders must travel through dangerous mountain passes and scorching deserts. They're never safe, for there's always the danger of thieves who wait to ambush them.

The man dropped a chunk of the hardened resin into a clay pot, where it warmed to a thick liquid the color of gold. Its perfume drifted to us in smoky wisps that smelled like lemons and musk.

"It was freshly harvested this spring," he said with pride. "With my own hands I slit the bark and held the bowls beneath to catch the oozing treasure."

The merchants love to tell stories of their travels, and it's one of the reasons I long to come when the trade caravans saunter through. I've heard tales of kings and queens and foreign lands I can only visit in my dreams. We listened as the merchant talked to the old woman.

"Come closer," he told her. "Do not fear. While this frankincense burns, evil spirits are kept at bay. Oh, you would not believe what my eyes have seen and my ears have heard!" His little eyes danced, and his arms moved through the air with the quickness and grace of a snake charmer I'd seen once.

"Palaces are scented with frankincense. It's true!" he told her. "After royal banquets, a pot of glowing embers is passed around the room to all of the guests. The men hold it beneath their chins to scent their jeweled beards. Women wave the perfumed smoke into their hair and silk robes."

He noticed that his audience had grown, and he waved to us to move near. "Come closer. Come closer," he called. "I am in good spirits today, and I will bestow a gift upon you." We walked toward him, and he took the clay pot and waved it around our heads. "Now the evil that has clung to your skin like a black veil will leave you. It is your lucky day."

We found Papa not long after that, and we left. We walked Ruth to her door, and Papa gave her a sack of grain. He had traded our wool for two sacks of grain, and he was kind and generous to give one away. Ruth had bartered an embroidered scarf for a basket of dates, and she filled a smaller basket with more than half of them for us.

She kissed me on the forehead before I left. "It was an enchanting day, Abi. It lifted my spirits, and for that I thank you."

Zibby was waiting for us in the courtyard when we returned. As soon as she heard our voices and our footsteps, she limped toward us, her tail wagging with joy. When Papa had moved ahead, I offered her a date, and to my surprise, she ate it. It's good nourishment for her, but I suspect that everyone in our home is nourishing our Zibby.

I think I'll sleep here on the roof tonight. The air is pleasant and the wind is light. The frankincense still clings to me, and I keep lifting my hair to my nose. Who would have thought I would be wearing the perfume of queens? It was an unusual day, and I haven't been able to get the merchant's words out of my head. *Now the evil that has clung to your skin like a black veil will leave you. It is your lucky day.* I wonder what that means.

One Week Later

Zibby's leg is much better! Today she whined and panted and barked and howled so convincingly that Papa allowed her to go into the fields with them. He slapped his leg, and Zibby took off running. She has just a trace of a limp now, but I don't know what shape she'll be in when she returns.

They'll be gone for at least two days as they graze the flocks in the uplands farther north.

A Widow's Tears

What a terrible time for Papa and the boys to be gone. Ruth ran to our house this morning, and in the time it took me to climb down the ladder from the roof, she collapsed in Mama's arms in a puddle of tears.

"You can't mean she intends to go by herself?" Mama was saying when I found them.

"Yes," Ruth sobbed. "She heard there is bread in Bethlehem. It's too hard for her in Moab now. It's hard for all of us now that our men are gone." I knelt down beside them and stroked Ruth's hand.

"When?" Mama asked. "When does she intend to do this?"

"I don't know; she won't say. She just cries and gnashes her teeth. I've never seen her so unhappy. She even told Orpah and me that we must call her Mara now. She says her name is no longer Naomi."

"What?" Mother cried. "Why would she say such a thing?"

"She said Mara means 'bitter,'" Ruth explained through her tears, "and that it's a more suitable name for her now. She said her Lord Almighty has afflicted her and brought misfortune upon her."

Ruth left not long after she came. She was too worried about Naomi to stay for long. Mama made her promise that she'd try to convince Naomi to stay put until the men returned.

The Next Day

Papa and my brothers returned today as expected with Zibby flying behind them. She was running so fast, the fur on her body was plastered to her skin. I heard her barking in the distance, and I went outside to see her racing the wind. She herded the flocks into the pen, dashing this way and that until they were inside. Then she ran to the water cistern and pushed her way between two sheep to satisfy her thirst. Ahmed was beaming with joy, and Asher and Papa were chuckling.

I whistled to Zibby. Her head shot up, and her tail flipped back and forth at high speed. I could have sworn she was smiling. In two seconds she'd reached me. She knocked me to the ground in her excitement, and she licked my face.

Mama stood by the door and laughed. "Come on, everyone, and that includes you, Zibby. It's time for supper."

We ate soup with red lentils, eggplant stuffed with grains, and fresh bread. I've never heard of a dog who eats vegetables and soup, but Zibby does. Mama scooped the leftovers into her bowl, and she ate her supper like she hadn't eaten in days.

Afterward, she curled up on the rug Mama set out for her in the courtyard. She was asleep within minutes. A moment ago I watched her twitch and tremble in her dreams. I think she was still running with the herds!

Papa said he'll visit Naomi and the girls again first thing in the morning. Mama told him what happened, and he's troubled. We all are.

A Sudden Surprise

Oh, diary! My life is about to change forever. In the span of one short morning, all that's familiar to me has been shaken like a skin of milk jostled into butter. I feel frantic with fear and worry, yet there's also a spring of excitement bubbling up inside me. How can this be?

I've never seen such a display of love as I saw today. When I told Mama what happened, she wept, and even Papa had tears in his eyes. I'll try to remember every detail here so it will be recorded forever. My memory will fail me one day, but as Ahmed has told me many times, the written word is immortalized.

I ran ahead to Naomi's house this morning, knowing that Mama and Papa would follow shortly. When I arrived the door was ajar, but no one answered when I called. I thought I heard Naomi's voice drift to me from the road, so I followed its lead. There she was, standing in the middle of a dirt path, flanked by Ruth and Orpah.

The three of them were in tears, and I stood there helpless, watching and listening.

Naomi touched them on their arms. "Go back, each of you, to your mother's home. May the LORD show kindness to you, as you have shown to your dead and to me. May the LORD grant that each of you will find rest in the home of another husband." She gave a tender kiss to each of them.

"No!" Ruth cried. "We will go back with you to your people."

Naomi shook her head. "Return home, my daughters. Why would you come with me? Am I going to have more sons, who could become your husbands? Return home, my daughters; I am too old to have another husband. Even if I thought there was still hope for me—even if I had a husband tonight and then gave birth to sons—would you wait until they grew up? Would you remain unmarried for them? No, my daughters. It is more bitter for me than for you, because the LORD's hand has gone out against me!"

Orpah kissed her mother-in-law good-bye, but Ruth clung to her.

"Look," Naomi told her, "your sister-in-law is going back to her people and her gods. Go back with her."

Ruth shook her head fiercely. "Don't urge me to leave you or to turn back from you," she sobbed. "Where you go I will go, and where you stay I will stay. Your people will be my people and your God my God. Where you die I will die, and there I will be buried. May the LORD deal with me, be it ever so severely, if anything but death separates you and me."

Orpah had left already, and I ran home as well. In my haste to tell Mama what had happened, I tripped several times and bloodied my hands and knees. Then Mama and I hurried to the fields to find Papa and tell him the story.

"Asher!" Papa called. "Run ahead. Naomi and Ruth are on the road to Bethlehem. Tell them we'll meet them at their first night's stop. Tell them to look for us."

My brother's eyes widened, but he said nothing.

"Ahmed, get the flocks in order," Papa commanded. "We will leave in a few hours' time."

To Mama he said, "We discussed the possibility of this, but now that the time is nigh, are you sure this is what you want?" My mother didn't hesitate before she nodded, and that surprised me. "Then take Abi back to the house and explain it to her. I must help Ahmed."

Mama told me that Papa feels an obligation to Naomi now that her sons and husband are gone. "Is that why Ruth won't leave her?" I asked. "Because she feels an obligation to care for her?"

"I believe so, "Mama said. "But it's more than that. Do you remember the prediction I made not long ago when I said Ruth would never leave Naomi?"

"Yes," I told her. "How did you know, Mama? How did you know this day would come and that Ruth wouldn't leave her?"

"It's one thing to leave your country when you

have no other choices," she explained. "Elimelech brought Naomi here when there was famine in Judah. Now there is the promise of bread there. She must return. She's old, and she's without any kin in a strange land. At least she will be comforted by the soil of her homeland, the presence of her God, and the promise of better things to come."

"But how did you know Ruth would go with her?" I asked.

"Ruth is a rare woman, Abi. She had the same devotion for her husband. Mahlon wasn't well thought of in Moab because he was an Israelite, yet she stood by his side and defended his honor. She possesses a faithfulness and devotion I've never seen before.

"Look at what she's doing," Mama continued. "She hasn't just agreed to accompany Naomi, she has chosen to leave behind her gods in order to serve Naomi's Lord. She has volunteered to leave her homeland forever."

Mama said she and Papa can't, in good conscience, allow Naomi and Ruth to make the journey alone. If anything happened to them, they wouldn't be able to forgive themselves.

It's Almost Time

The flocks are ready for their journey, as is Zibby. We can't bring much—just an extra change of clothes, food for the journey, skins of water, and a few miscellaneous things. Of course, I will take you, my dear diary, and my pens. Nothing can separate me from you.

Papa said there are fields outside Bethlehem where he hopes to set up a tent. It's not a large tent, just one he uses when he takes the flocks out for longer stretches. We'll stay long enough to see Naomi and Ruth settled, he told us. Of course, he said he doesn't know how long that will be.

I admit to feeling afraid. Is this how Naomi felt when she came to Moab? Elimelech told her one day, "There is famine in our land. Come, we must leave our home and journey to Moab." Did they take only what they could carry on their journey, not knowing where they would live or how they would find food?

Orpah will stay in Naomi's house. She seems sad that everyone is leaving, but I can tell she doesn't regret her decision. Mama said it won't be long before she remarries and has children. Papa left her with more than half our grain, as well as two goats and two sheep. She'll always have milk, butter, cheese, and yogurt. If necessary, she'll have meat as well.

I forgot to tell you that Papa surprised me with new papyrus sheets from Egypt. I don't know what he traded to get these, but I know the wool couldn't have bought the grain as well as the paper. When I asked him, he just winked at me. I'm so happy and grateful. Paper is to me like frankincense is to a queen! If I'm careful, I'll have enough for two fresh diaries. I can use one to record our crossing from Moab to Israel, and the other can be used when we reach our new home in the village of Bethlehem.

Oh, it's time to leave. Ahmed just called to me. We have to reach Naomi and Ruth before nightfall, he said. For some reason, the name of Naomi's God has been in my head today. He has many names, Naomi once told me, but the one I hear her use most is *Yahweh-jereh*. She said it means "Yahweh provides." I've always liked that the sound of that. I suppose it brings me peace on this day of great uncertainty.

Diary Two

The Crossing
Moab to Israel

Day One ~ The Road North

We've reached the end of day one on our journey to Israel, and am I glad! I can't complain out loud, because it would be rude, and Mama says grumbling serves no purpose. I know she's right, but I can't help but feel miserable about my aching feet.

Papa said that starting tomorrow he'll pace us so we'll walk the same distance every day. Today was a longer day than usual because we got off to such a late start. I just took off my sandals a few minutes ago. Two gaping blisters, one on each foot, have been rubbed raw and bloody. How will I ever be able to walk tomorrow?

We left Dibon on the king's highway and headed north. There were no friends or family to bid us farewell. Instead, we passed a field of graves where some of our ancestors are buried. Elimelech and his sons lie in shallow tombs, but

I didn't look when we walked by. I didn't want to feel sadder than I already was.

Zibby herded the flocks well, and she made sure none of them wandered away. She was also a great comfort to me; every once in a while I felt her wet nose nudge my hand. I think she was trying to encourage me.

Toward the end of the day, when I thought I couldn't walk another step, we spotted Naomi and Ruth. Their blankets were spread beside an acacia tree, and the smiles on their faces revealed their gratitude and relief. Ruth jumped up to hug me tight, and even bitter Naomi put her arms around me when I bent down to greet her.

"Why have you come?" she asked Mama and Papa. "There's no need for you to do this thing. God is calling me home, but my home is not yours."

Papa told Naomi that he was obliged to see that she and Ruth made the journey safely and that they were settled and cared for. His next words surprised me, and I think they surprised Asher and Ahmed as well—"This country is no longer our home, Naomi. Many of our neighbors have turned against us, and our gods don't seem to notice our plight."

I want to talk to Papa about this, but not tonight; I'm too tired. My brothers are keeping a close watch on the flocks because thieves wander these roads. Papa is staying close to us to protect us for the same reason. I'm so glad. I feel safe when he's near.

We're lucky that it's spring. The winter rains left many pockets of water underground, and they're easily found by digging. The shadows are growing long as the day melts away, so we've spread out our blankets. I'll have to stop writing in a moment.

Naomi just reached into her bag and pulled out a small pouch of honey, which she dabbed on my open blisters. "When we're close to the Salt Sea, we'll stop and take a dip," she told me. "Your wounds will heal more quickly, and all of our aching bodies will benefit."

Even through her sorrow and her exhaustion, she's kind and compassionate like Ruth. I wish I were more like them. When I'm weary and don't feel well, I want to bark like Zibby. I know I must learn to control my temper.

Tomorrow will be a long day. Asher said we'll descend from the hills through a narrow gorge that leads to the sea. Ruth touched my hand and told me to lie down between her and Mama. I will. The dawn will come too soon, and I need to sleep.

Day Two ~ The Salt Sea

I'm sitting on my blanket, gazing at the sea. My outstretched legs aren't more than twenty paces from the shore. What an eerie sight. A blue haze hangs over the water like a tent canopy. Papa said it's caused by the water that's drawn out of the sea into the air.

Huge boulders of pure salt are left scattered around the shore when the water has evaporated. They sparkle like diamonds against a cloudless blue sky. Salt pillars even grow out of the water. They look like dead, white tree stumps. Traders carry the salt from this sea to faraway lands where the mineral isn't so plentiful.

The mountains surrounding the sea are bleached white like wool. Their backs are not smooth, grassy hills but naked knobs and peaks where trees and flowers are afraid to grow.

We reached the sea about an hour ago and had to pick our way around the dead, stinking fish that wash up on the shore. The Jordan River runs into the Salt Sea and sends the poor fish to their death. They can't live in such salty water. Not much can, but at least the wild animals can feed on the fish. At least their lives aren't a complete waste.

All of us, except my brothers, floated in the water for a time. Asher and Ahmed led the flocks away from the salt water, which isn't good for them to drink. The water is clear, which is surprising, but it has a terrible taste. Zibby discovered that when she lapped at the waves. She shook her head repeatedly as if to shake the bitter taste from her tongue, and then she whined and ran off. She was so disappointed, she didn't even cool her tired, sore paws in the sea.

Swimming was great fun, but I had to take care not to splash in the water or splash anyone around me. The minerals are so strong, they'll burn your eyes. I floated upright with the water tucked beneath my armpits. I sat with my legs outstretched, and I even reclined on my back, as if on my bed mat, with both my head and my heels afloat above the water. When I swam, I had to concentrate to keep my feet from flying out the water. I don't think I could drown if I tried.

The water was oily, and it felt as though I was swimming in a vat of slime. The sea left a thin layer of salt on our skin, and the scorching heat dried our bodies to a powdery white.

At first my blisters screamed with pain when I dipped my toes into the sea. I cried from the sting of salt in my open wounds, but now they feel much better. Naomi was right. Salt cleans sores and helps them heal. I will wrap each of the afflicted toes with a piece of soft cloth before we walk again tomorrow.

It's a good thing we arrived here late in the day and will leave with the moonlight to guide us early in the morning. We're sunk deep in a valley, and the heat is trapped between the mountains. There isn't even the slightest hint of a breeze to ripple the calm water. Papa says we can't stay long here. The glare from the white hills will burn our skin and roast us like locusts. Of course, he exaggerates, but I've heard stories of travelers who have died here.

We waited to build a fire until the moon lit our camp. I'm lucky to have enough light to write. Naomi made bread in the hot ashes, and we pulled out the dates Ruth bartered for when we visited the trade caravans. Dibon seems so far away from this strange, white land of nothingness. A simple meal of bread and dates never tasted so good. It's the same thing we ate yesterday, but no one cares.

Later

I just remembered! I saw something interesting earlier today that I don't want to forget to write down. Naomi pointed out Mount Nebo this morning. She said this is the mountain where her God led Moses before the Israelites entered Canaan. Moses wasn't allowed to enter their Promised Land because he had sinned, but God wanted to show him the beauty of the land he had given them. Then Moses died. She said an angel buried his body in a secret grave, which no one has been able to find!

If he lies on the mountain somewhere, I think it's a beautiful resting place. The land he led his people to is spread out below him, and the deep gorges at the foot of Mount Nebo are green with pomegranate trees and dotted orange with their juicy fruit.

I had a chance to talk with Papa today while Mama walked ahead with Ruth and Naomi. "Do you think their God really parted the Red Sea for Moses like the Israelites say?" I asked him.

He nodded his head at once. "Yes, I have no reason to doubt it. Their God has done miraculous things since the time of Abraham. Remember, he promised Sarah a son when she was barren, and she bore one at the old age of ninety!"

"Have our gods ever done miracles like that?"

Papa was silent for a moment as he walked. No," he admitted. "Not that I'm aware of."

I've been thinking about this all day. We have many gods, but has anyone seen them or heard their voices? I've always liked the story of Beelphegor. Mama has told it to me many times. It goes like this:

A long time ago Beelphegor was the storm god. He brought rain to the land, which made the crops grow. The gods were jealous of one another, and there was an argument between Beelphegor and Yamm, the god of the sea. Beelphegor called upon his sister Anat, the goddess of war, and Astarte, the goddess of the earth and fertility. With their help, Beelphegor de-feated Yamm as well as Tannin, the dragon of the sea, and Loran, the serpent with seven heads.

The other gods agreed to build a splendid house for Beelphegor so he could rest in comfort and give rain to the earth. One day, Mot, the god of death, challenged Beelphegor. Mot won, and Beelphegor sank into the depths of the underworld. His sister Anat and Shapash, the sun god, flew to the underworld and searched everywhere until they found him. They brought him back to life, and he returned to live in his splendid house, where he was worshiped as the leader of the gods.

There is also a poem, which was written a very long time ago:

And the club danced in Baal's hands,
like a vulture from his fingers.
It struck Prince Sea on the skull,
Judge River between the eyes.
Sea stumbled; He fell to the ground;
his joints shook;
his frame collapsed
Baal captured and drank Sea;
he finished off Judge River.
Astarte shouted Baal's name:
"Hail, Baal the Conqueror!
Hail, Rider on the Clouds!
For Prince Sea is our captive,
Judge River is our captive."

I'm wondering now if it's really a true story or just a myth. I suppose there's no way to know.

It's time to sleep. Ruth just tapped on my hand with her finger and smiled at me. Mama's look was not so sweet. There will be much for me to think about as we continue our trek toward Jericho. Long journeys on foot give your mind time to ponder. I think I've learned this trait from Ahmed.

Day Three ~ Jericho

We've just arrived! The day is still young, so we'll have more time to rest than usual. Thank goodness! Everyone is weary.

Papa woke us like he said he would, a few hours before sunrise. We left the desolation of the Salt Sea behind us, but we wandered farther into the Judean wilderness. It's a harsh desert, and if it weren't for the Jordan River and the oasis at Jericho, I don't think we would have survived.

We've been very lucky on our journey so far. The snows of Mount Herman to the north haven't fully melted and run off into the lakes and rivers to the south. If we'd waited one more week, the runoff would have swelled the Jordan River and we may not have found a shallow spot to cross. We found a narrow ford this morning about twenty cubits across, and the deepest part reached only to my waist.

The water was dirty and yellow, but it felt wonderful after my swim in the Salt Sea. My tunic had dried stiff, my skin was dry and itchy, and my hair felt coarse like hay. The river water didn't soften our skin like olive oil would, but it did wash away the salt residue.

The Jordan is lined with oleander bushes that are blossoming with fragrant pink and white flowers. After we bathed we refilled our skins and rested in the soft grasses. Zibby was excited. When the sheep and goats had crossed and were busy grazing, she darted back to the river and swam back and forth several times. Then she climbed onto the shore and sprayed all of us as she cheerfully shook herself.

Mama was deep in conversation with Naomi,

so I sat next to Ruth. I let my bare feet and calves dangle in the water while I rested my back on the bank.

"Ruth?"

"Mm-hmm," she murmured. Her eyes were closed, but I knew she wasn't asleep. Her fingers were tapping lightly on her stomach.

"Are you afraid?" I asked.

She turned on her side and rested her head on her hand. "Yes," she admitted. "I'm afraid, but I'm also peaceful. I feel both at the same time, if that makes sense."

"Won't you miss Moab?"

"Of course," she replied, "but I couldn't leave Naomi. How could I, Abi? She's lost so much—first her homeland, then her husband, and now her children."

"Yes," I agreed, "but now you've lost so much. Your husband died, and now you've left the homeland of your ancestors and your gods."

Ruth told me that she's young enough to begin again. "Sometimes you have to let go of that which is comfortable and familiar in order to make a new life for yourself," she said. "Courage isn't courage if you have nothing to fear, right?"

She placed her hand over mine and squeezed it. "I'm a Moabite, and yet Naomi accepted me as her daughter-in-law without question. She loved me unconditionally like a daughter. Now it's my turn to honor her like a mother. Did you know that's one of the laws God gave to Moses—to honor your mother and father?"

I was so surprised, I couldn't think of words.

Ruth laughed. "I was married to an Israelite," she reminded me. "I learned much about their God. In some ways I feel more like an Israelite than a Moabite."

Papa said it was time to move on, so I couldn't finish my conversation with Ruth. Once again I was left with much to think about.

The flocks are grazing beside us now in the oasis at Jericho, so Asher and Ahmed have fallen asleep. They've left Zibby in charge for a short while. She dances around the animals and barks at their heels when they wander too far. It looks

like the others will nap for a short while, so I think
I'll join them.

Later

No one awakened refreshed from their nap today.
I, for one, am irritable and sore, and my spirits are
low. How is it that the promise of bread in Israel
that Naomi speaks of can only be reached by a
journey through such a harsh wilderness? How
many travelers have died on this road before they
reached their destination?

My two blisters are healing, but three new ones
have already erupted to take their place. I never
knew it was possible to be so weary that even a
paradise like Jericho can't erase your memories
and your fears of the wilderness all around you.

Scrub brush dotted the desert between the
Jordan River and Jericho. Once in a while we
came across a sumac bush. A green bush in the
wilderness! What a treat for our eyes! Its red,
hairy fruit and feathery leaves were beautiful and

interesting in comparison to the stark hills and brown desert floor.

We saw Jericho's date palms from a long ways away. Their tall, brown trunks and green fronds waved to us from the blue sky and welcomed us to their oasis like long lost kin. Golden red dates hung in juicy clusters. We spread our blankets on a rug of thick, green grass beneath the boughs of a broad sycamore fig tree.

A large spring bubbles up from beneath the ground, which is why an oasis exists in the middle of the wilderness. The flocks were watered, and everyone except Ruth and me was allowed to drink the fresh, clean water.

There is a curse on the water, Papa told us, and any woman who drinks from it will not bear children. Since Mama and Naomi won't have more babies, they drank from it freely. Ruth and I drank from the water of the Jordan River that remains in our skins. It's dirty, but if it quenched our thirst then, I suppose it will have to quench our thirst now. What can we do?

Not far from the small oasis lie the ruins of the

great city that once stood here. Its burned rubble is scattered across a high mound like broken tombs. Everywhere we go on this journey, I come face-to-face with Naomi's God. It was here that Joshua led the Israelites and their priests around the city. They marched, they blew rams' horns, and they shouted until the walls collapsed.

"How did your God do this?" I asked Naomi. Jericho was a mighty fortress with walls many cubits thick. It was built to withstand armies charging with battering rams.

"With God all things are possible," she replied.

"But why didn't the gods of the Canaanites stop your God?" I cried. "Surely the people must have cried out to their gods for help."

"For the same reason Abraham stopped worshiping many gods and declared the sovereignty of the one true God," Naomi explained. "He realized that those gods have no real power. Ours is the only living God."

The Israelites conquered the city and burned it, and then Joshua put a curse on anyone who tried to rebuild it. Papa says it has been a graveyard of ashes ever since. Our gods do seem small and helpless in comparison.

A few minutes ago Papa handed me a persimmon to feast on. I'm happy to say that it has cheered me somewhat. Persimmons are reddish-orange fruits that are a bit plump. They taste as smooth and sweet as honey. Just now he set down a handful of ripe figs, dates, and oranges. This is one spot of good news. Papa always knows how to put a smile on my face!

Now for the bad news: Jericho is deep in the Judean wilderness. I fear the journey between here and Bethlehem will be harder than ever. The hills are filled with natural limestone caves, which are home to lions and bears. Bandits also lurk in the shadows.

We're still sunk in the same valley that holds the Salt Sea captive. In order to get to Bethlehem, we must climb out of the valley through a pass called the "ascent of blood." The Jericho Road will take us the rest of the way.

Day Four ~ The Judean Desert

My emotions are up and down, much like the hills and valleys we've trekked through over the last few days. I'm tired of thinking. I'm more like my brother Ahmed than I thought—always thinking, always wondering, always filled with questions no one can answer.

Papa says we might reach Bethlehem tomorrow! He said it's a beautiful place with rich pastures for the flocks, vineyards, and many olive groves. We'll enter our new home (who knows how long we'll stay) at the start of the barley harvest. This is the promise of bread Naomi speaks of every day.

Right now, though, Bethlehem seems far away and unreachable. I woke up this morning with a pit of fear in my stomach. Will we wander through this wilderness forever? We are Moabites, after all. Perhaps this promise of bread is meant for Naomi and not for us.

We'd hoped to reach Yerushalayim today, but our climb out of the valley took us longer than we expected. It was far more exhausting than we could have realized. Ahmed reminded Papa that Jericho is more than five hundred cubits *below* sea level and Yerushalayim is more than sixteen hundred cubits *above* sea level. Travel was treacherous. We began our journey this morning in a hole, and we had to climb out of it before we could begin the normal ascent.

We left in the cool of the night again. Ruth held Naomi's hand and gently encouraged her when she grew tired. I held Mama's, but I'll admit that Mama encouraged me more than I encouraged her. The black tents and campfire smoke of bedouin camps rose against the steep, white cliffs, and that comforted me. I knew that if we ran out of water or had trouble in any way, the nomads would welcome us into their homes and help us.

The trail along the sharp embankments was so narrow at times that we had to walk in single file. Papa and my brothers guided the flocks up one by one, worried the whole time that one of the animals would fall off a ledge. None did, and that may have been thanks to Zibby, who followed in the rear.

We passed many caves, and I was reminded of the lions and bears and bandits that could be lurking within. I crept past, my heart pounding hard inside my chest. I was sure I saw a dark shadow in the entrance of one cave, and I even heard Zibby snarl as she trotted by. The hair on my arms stood on end, and little bumps prickled on my skin. Papa sensed my fear and called out, "A shadow is like a ghost, Abi. It can't harm you. It brings fear, but when you shine light on it, you realize there's nothing there to worry about."

I was glad to leave the ascent of blood if for no other reason than the threat of its name, but the Jericho Road wasn't much better. The slopes between Jericho and Yerushalayim are so steep, the rain clouds and west winds are shut out most of the year.

We walked for several hours and spotted little more than desert plants like the salt bush, the bitter wild onion, the caper, and the asphodel, which has edible roots. Papa pulled a small knife from his pocket and dug out a plant he called thumbling thistle. He cut and peeled the stalks and offered us the juicy part inside.

Mama looked at him skeptically.

"I'm a shepherd, dear wife," he reminded her. "I know how to survive in the wilderness."

We all ate a bit of the plant, which was wet and refreshed our dry tongues but tasted like sour grass. He peeled several more stalks, and Zibby eagerly licked the juices.

As we climbed, the small desert plants gave way to shrubs and later trees. We're camped under several trees right now. It looks like we've survived the worst part of our journey, but I'm too tired to feel victorious. We saw no bandits and no dangerous animals, and all of our flock survived. Naomi said her God protected us. In the past, Papa would have made a sarcastic comment under his breath. I noticed that today he said nothing. I caught Ruth's eye, and she winked at me.

This may be my last entry in this diary if we reach Bethlehem tomorrow. I suppose it's fitting that I begin a new diary for another new phase of my life. I'm ready to put this one behind me for good.

Diary Three

Spring in Bethlehem

The Promise of Bread

We arrived in Bethlehem in Judah as a light mist fell from the sky. Oh, to breathe in moist air! In the last day or so, I developed a cough, which Mama says is caused by breathing in the dry dust of the desert. Asher's eyes are red and swollen for the same reason, and though Mama doesn't say so, I know she's worried they'll grow worse.

Bethlehem means "promise of bread," and I can see why. We came just in time for the barley harvest, and the air is fragrant with the scent of earthy barley. Oxen with weighted sleds trampled the fields, and in doing so they separated the grain from the stalks

We passed several threshing floors, which are enormous piles of grain. Men dug their winnowing forks into the piles and tossed the grain into the air. In this way, Papa told me, the chaff—which is seed coverings and other debris—was separated from the grain. The grain is threshed and win-nowed late in the day and throughout the night when the air is cooler.

The terraced hills are also thick with olive groves, almond trees, and the famous vineyards, which will produce huge red grapes in the summer. It's a paradise in comparison to the wilderness we passed through the last few days, and my eyes can hardly take it in. Is it real? Perhaps it's just a dream and I'll awaken to find that I'm still climbing, climbing, climbing . . .

The road to Bethlehem from Yerushalayim was busy. We saw more people on this road in one day than we'd seen in all the days of our journey. Camels and donkeys were loaded with goods such as lime from the hills, and they passed each other in both directions. Some were traveling north to Yerushalayim and beyond; the others were headed south to Hebron or even Egypt. The men, women, and children were either on foot or on their donkeys.

I stared at them and tried to catch their eye. Could they tell I was a Moabite? My dress was a little different from theirs, although it didn't stand out that much. They didn't seem to notice me though, and I felt relieved. This was my great fear—that my family and even Ruth would be recognized as foreigners, or worse, enemies, and we would be shunned. It hasn't happened so far.

Papa found a field to graze the flocks and a shady spot by a grove of trees to pitch the tent. He stayed there with Ahmed and Asher while Mama and I walked into town with Naomi and Ruth. I don't think Naomi had any idea what to do. It was so long ago when she left, she wasn't even sure if anyone would remember her. She was wrong.

The roads in town were powdered white with the dust of the limestone used to make the buildings. We entered the town and turned left through the small bazaar. We passed a baker's shop, and the smell of warm bread and sweet cakes made me realize how hungry I was. Mama left me and was walking ahead when I heard a sudden commotion and loud voices. Naomi was surrounded by a group of people, and Mama and Ruth had been left outside the circle. I hurried closer.

"Naomi? Could it be you?" a woman asked.

I stood on my tiptoes and saw the face of the older woman who asked the question. She was dressed well in a pretty striped tunic, and her gray hair was braided and hung over her shoulder.

I looked down at my own dress and realized for the first time in days that we were dirty and very poor in comparison to the women who surrounded Naomi. We hadn't even bathed since we dipped ourselves in the Jordan River several days ago. My toes were brown with dust, and dirt clung to the dry cracks between my fingers. Mama must have realized the same thing, for I saw her run her hand over her hair in a self-conscious way.

"Don't call me Naomi," Naomi cried to the woman. "Call me Mara, because the Almighty has made my life very bitter."

I was shocked at her response and looked at Ruth. She was already gazing at me, and now she bent down. "I think these were Naomi's friends a long time ago. When she lived here with her husband, she was very well off and her life was filled with joy. I'm sure she wore fine clothes like they are wearing. She's bitter now because she's lost everything. Now she dresses like the people she once tossed coins to and pitied."

My eyes widened when she said this. "You mean, like the beggars?" I asked.

Ruth nodded. I could see sorrow in her eyes for the woman she wanted to protect but couldn't.

Naomi turned away from the women. "I went away full, but the LORD has brought me back empty," she moaned. "Why call me Naomi? The LORD has afflicted me; the Almighty has brought misfortune upon me."

I watched the crowd murmur as they watched her leave, but not a single one of them offered to help her. Naomi's shoulders were bent, and she seemed old to me for the first time. Ruth rushed forward and draped a protective arm over her shoulders. Mama told me later that Naomi knew the women weren't happy to see her. They were just nosey.

I'm sitting now in the tent my brothers set up while we were gone. Naomi and Ruth have decided to stay in town. A short while after Naomi left her old friends in the crowd, a woman named

Carmelina approached her. I'd seen her lurking in the shadows by the buildings. She was very old, and her skin was brown and loose. It hung from her bones in loose, wrinkled folds like a thin scarf.

She offered to let Naomi and Ruth stay in her home for as long as they needed to. Her husband had been dead for many years, she said, and while her home was very small, they were welcome to spread their blankets on the floor and stay with her.

"Did Naomi know this woman?" I asked Mama as we walked back to the fields on the outside of town.

"I don't know," she told me. "From what I could tell, Carmelina is very poor. When Naomi and Elimelech lived in Bethlehem, they were quite well off. The poor and the wealthy don't often spend time together."

I think it's sad that Naomi's rich friends aren't so nice now that Naomi isn't rich anymore. Yet a simple, poor woman was willing to take her in and offer her whatever she had.

I don't know what tomorrow or the next day holds. While all seems strange and foreign to me, at least I know we'll be here for more than a few hours. We aren't far from a huge rock cistern, so we've already found a water source. We'll need to haul more water to our camp so we can wash ourselves, but that won't be done until tomorrow. We're all too tired.

My tummy is content for now. We ate the last of the fruit we carried from Jericho, and Mama made a bit of bread. All our supplies are low, but at least we won't run out of goats' milk. Tomorrow I'll make butter and yogurt and cheese after we milk the flocks. That will be a real treat for all of us.

Late the Next Day ~ I'm Clean!

This morning I watched the sun rise over the distant Salt Sea. The white hills glowed orange and red, and the water reflected the rays like a shimmering mirror. Bethlehem is on a high ridge, so I can see far to the east and to the south where the hills slope sharply away. It's a constant reminder of where we were and how far we've traveled.

It's been a busy day. Papa and my brothers built a sheep pen out of rocks and branches, and Mama and I tried to make our tent feel like home. We strung up thin blankets and sectioned off the tent to make three small rooms: one in the front to eat and lounge in and two in the back to sleep in. Mama and I will share one sleeping room, and my brothers will share the other with Papa.

It's cozy in here now, and I feel more peaceful today than I've felt in many days. The pit of fear has finally left me. I walked several times to the cistern with Mama, and we hauled enough water to wash ourselves. The water dribbled off my skin in brown rivulets, and I was glad to see the dirt of our journey in the wilderness wash away. I feel fresh and clean again.

Mama helped me wash my hair. We had a bit of ash with us, which we used with the water to wash ourselves. When my hair was clean enough to squeak, she drizzled several drops of olive oil into it and massaged my scalp. I was so relaxed and content, I almost fell asleep.

Then I helped wash and moisturize Mama's hair. Her hair is longer than mine, and I hardly ever see it loose and unbraided. When she combed it out, it fell to her waist in a glossy sheet. I thought she was lovelier than I'd ever seen her. Papa came in from the field then, and when he saw her his eyes grew wide. Mama blushed, something I've never seen, and she shooed him away with a nervous little laugh.

Asher held Zibby for me, and I dumped some of the dirty water over her and rubbed her with some of the ash. She stunk last night. When she ran into the tent, an odor filled the air, and we groaned and held our noses until Ahmed shooed her out. Papa thinks she might have found the carcass of a dead animal. I don't want to think about what she did with it. I backed off before she could shake and spray me with her wet fur.

I didn't have time to make the butter, yogurt, and cheese as I'd planned, but there's always tomorrow. We didn't see Ruth or Naomi today, but

Mama says we'll give them some time to settle themselves. If they don't come by soon, we'll go into town and visit them at Carmelina's house.

Gleaning in the Fields

We didn't have to go to town after all. Ruth came by just past daybreak. Papa and my brothers were heading into the fields when she appeared in the doorway.

"Ruth! Come and sit down." Mama pointed to a thin mat on the floor. "The bread is still warm. Abi, get her some bread and goats' milk."

"No, no," Ruth told her. "I've already eaten." I wondered if she was just being polite. Carmelina couldn't have enough food to feed three people. I don't think she had enough food to feed herself most days.

"I've come to see if you'd allow Abi to glean in the fields with me."

"Glean in the fields?" Mama asked with one cocked eyebrow.

"Yes," Ruth told her. "The Israelites have a

wonderful law. It allows widows, the poor, and foreigners to pick up the grain that's dropped by the workers in the fields."

"How much do we have to pay for this grain?" Mama inquired.

"We pay with grateful hearts," Ruth replied with a smile. "This is a good country, Ketura. They try to help those in need. Of course, you have to be willing to humble yourself to glean in the fields. It isn't a job for those with proud hearts."

"Let me go with her, Mama," I cried. "It will put bread on our table." I ran to get the sack of grain and lifted it easily with a few fingers. "See? We don't have much left."

The dew was spread over the golden hills like butter on bread, and I felt the wet seep into my sandals as we walked. Ruth led me to one of the large fields beside the threshing floors we'd passed on the way to town. We stood for a moment and watched the activity. Women cut down the tall stalks with sickles and let them fall to the ground. Their hairlines were wet with perspiration, and they stopped often to rub the small of their backs.

The men followed behind, their muscles bulging as they gathered up the stalks and bundled them into loose sheaves. When all the grain was reaped, the field would become a threshing floor like the others we'd seen.

I followed Ruth through the field, careful not to step on the stalks lying here and there. I watched her search the faces of the curious men until she found one who appeared to be in charge. I stole a glance behind me as we walked, and I watched both the men and the women stare after her. Ruth is beautiful. Every time I'm with her, she attracts attention.

I remember the trade caravan on the king's highway in Dibon and the old merchant who gave her the glass beads. They were a token of his appreciation for her beauty.

"Please, sir," she said to the man in charge, "let us glean and gather among the sheaves behind the harvesters."

The man looked at her for a long moment, and

I held my breath. "You're the Moabitess, aren't you. The one who accompanied Naomi from Moab." He spoke the words like a conclusion rather than a question.

"I am Ruth of Moab," she answered.

He nodded, and I watched his eyes drift in my direction as he took notice of me for the first time. Ruth reached for my hand, and before he could speak she said, "This is my friend, Abi. She is a Moabite also."

"Go on, then. You may glean," he told us. "Of course, Boaz, the owner, will have the final say when he comes to the fields later today. You'll meet him, I'm sure."

Ruth lowered her eyes and whispered her thanks.

She'd brought two huge baskets that Carmelina gave her to use, and she handed one to me. I'd never gleaned before, and I don't think Ruth had either, but for the next few hours, we stooped in the dirt and gathered the stalks of grain that had fallen here and there.

The sun was high in the sky before we looked

up from our task. Ruth touched my arm. "Come into the shade for a few minutes," she whispered. "There's a worker who stares at us. I don't trust him. We'll let him move ahead for a little while."

I looked up casually and saw the man Ruth spoke of. He jeered when he saw me look up, and I noticed that several of his teeth were missing. He gathered a bundle of wheat and stared at us for longer than he should have.

"If he continues like this, we'll go to another field the next time," Ruth told me.

I nodded. The man frightened me, but my thirst was my biggest concern. We'd forgotten to bring water, and already my throat was dry. The roof of my mouth stuck to my tongue in an uncomfortable way.

The breeze beneath the trees cooled the drops of sweat that trickled down my neck, but I felt discouraged. I'd had no idea gleaning was such hard work. My back ached, and my knees popped from the constant bending.

"Can you go on?" Ruth asked me softly. Her

cheeks were flushed, and her eyes were weary. "I hoped to gather at least a basketful of grain today. What do you think?"

I looked into our baskets. We'd worked so long, yet our baskets were only half full. I forced a smile for her and nodded, but I quickly turned away. I felt the prickle of hot tears in my eyes.

There's much more to tell, but I'll finish in the morning. My back is screaming at me to lie on my mat and sleep, and my hand can hardly hold my pen upright, the muscles ache so.

The Next Day ~ The Handsome Owner

I thought I was sore last night, but how wrong I was. This morning I awakened stiff like a board. Mama heated some rocks in the fire and wrapped them in cloth. Right now they're under my legs, but the next batch will be under by back, warming my muscles so they'll relax. To continue my story . . .

Ruth and I rested for just a short while before returning to the fields. The workers sang while they worked, and I liked it. Their songs were about their God, and they were beautiful and peaceful. They helped take my mind off my work. I was so lost in thought that I jumped when a deep voice called out, "The LORD be with you!"

A man stood at the edge of the field. He was tall, and he had broad shoulders and a kind face. "It must be the owner, Boaz," Ruth told me. The harvesters called back to him, "The LORD bless you!"

Boaz turned to the man Ruth had spoken to earlier, and they both looked in our direction. Boaz walked toward us, but Ruth kept her head low and averted her eyes.

"My daughter, listen to me," he said to Ruth. "Don't go and glean in another field and don't go away from here. Stay here with my servant girls. Watch the field where the men are harvesting, and follow along after the girls. I have told the men not to touch you. And whenever you are thirsty, go and get a drink from the water jars the men have filled."

Ruth bowed low with her face to the ground. "Why have I found such favor in your eyes that you notice me—a foreigner?" she asked in a trembling voice.

Boaz smiled tenderly. "I've been told all about what you have done for your mother-in-law since the death of your husband—how you left your father and mother and your homeland and came to live with a people you did not know before."

He looked at me then. "And you, Abi. Your family has come to Israel to look after Naomi and Ruth. May the Lord repay both of you for what you have done. May you be richly rewarded by the LORD, the God of Israel, under whose wings you have come to take refuge."

"May we continue to find favor in your eyes, my lord," Ruth replied. "You have given us comfort and spoken kindly to your servants—though we do not have the standing of your servant girls."

Boaz left, but a short while later we noticed

that the worker who had been staring at us had disappeared from the fields. We didn't see him again for the rest of the day. Later, when my stomach told me it was time for supper, Boaz came to us. "Come over here. Have some bread and dip it in the wine vinegar."

We sat down with the harvesters, and he offered us roasted grain as well. It was the first meal I'd eaten since morning, and I'd begun to feel faint with hunger. We ate until we were full, and when we left to return to the fields, I heard Boaz say to the men, "Even if she gathers among the sheaves, don't embarrass her. Rather, pull out some stalks for her from the bundles and leave them for her to pick up, and don't rebuke her."

He was talking about Ruth, but she didn't hear him. She was already well ahead of me. We gleaned until the evening when our baskets were full, and then when I thought we were ready to return home, Ruth walked to the edge of the field and picked up two sticks. She handed one to me. "Now we must beat the grain from the stalks," she said wearily.

When all of the grain had fallen to the ground, we took our hands and tossed it into the air. Our pile was too small to use a winnowing fork. The breeze carried away the chaff, and we scooped the remaining barley into our baskets. They weren't even half full, and I felt my spirits sink. Ruth seemed pleased, but to me it was a pitiful day's work.

Before we left, Boaz called to us, "Return to the fields tomorrow and the next day. Stay with my workers until they have finished harvesting all my grain."

I felt his eyes watching us, or rather Ruth, until he lost sight of us beyond the hill. The field isn't far from our camp, so Ruth walked me home, and in turn, Ahmed accompanied her to town.

Zibby greeted me with her tail wagging to and fro. I wrapped my arms around her warm, soft neck and hugged her tight, and she licked my face and barked her greetings in my ear. What a friend and a comfort she is to me. She's always happy to see me, and I her. I reached into my pocket and pulled out a piece of bread and a handful of the roasted grain left over from my supper.

I thought Mama would be disappointed with my bushel of grain, but I was wrong. I've never seen someone cry and laugh all at once. Papa and my brothers couldn't believe their eyes.

"Imagine that," Asher said, "the youngest one brings home bread in a strange land!"

I'll return to the fields tomorrow with Ruth, but to tell the truth, I don't look forward to it. I dread it. There's at least one advantage that makes my misery worthwhile—I'm getting special treatment. I don't know how long it will last, so I think I should take advantage of it!

Mama has heated rocks for me again, and she plans to make porridge tonight for the first time since we left Moab. She said I have to stay well nourished or I'll become ill. I haven't had to do my usual chores today either!

I keep thinking about what Boaz said to Ruth and me. His words play in my mind over and over again. May you be richly rewarded by the LORD, the God of Israel, under whose wings you have come to take refuge.

Is that what we did when we came here? We

took refuge under the wings of the God of Israel? Did we know we'd done that? Will the God of Israel allow strangers like us to find protection under his wings? If he does, then I think he's a great God. Perhaps he's even greater than our gods.

The Gold of the Day

When the new sun shines on the barley fields and a light wind blows the stalks, the land looks like a sea of gold from the distance. It makes it easier to rise so early when my body aches and my mouth wants to complain. I've returned from another long day in the fields. This one was no easier than the first, but at least I felt free to drink the water and rest in the shade when the heat of the day was upon us.

Ruth brought interesting news this morning. When she told Naomi that the man she worked with was called Boaz, Naomi said, "The LORD bless him. He has not stopped showing kindness to the living and the dead. That man is our close relative; he is one of our kinsman-redeemers."

I asked Ruth what it means to be a kinsman-redeemer, and she told me that she didn't know at first either and that Naomi had to explain it to her. "In Israel," Ruth told me, "there's a law that allows the closest relatives of the dead to take care of their widows. Boaz is related to Elimelech, and Naomi is Elimelech's widow, and since I'm the widow of Elimelech's son, I suppose Boaz is responsible for me too."

She continued, "Naomi doesn't believe it's a coincidence that brought me to the one field that belongs to her dead husband's relative."

"If it wasn't a coincidence, then what was it?" I asked her.

"Well," Ruth said thoughtfully, "perhaps God guides my footsteps after all."

"You mean Naomi's God?"

"I mean my God, Abi—the God of Israel. The God who doesn't demand that we sacrifice children in his name or send our women to dance in his temples. I believe now that he is the one true God."

Once again the harvesters sang praises to their

God all day as they worked. Their words stay in my head, and I often hum their tunes as I walk home late in the evening. They're even on my lips when I rise in the morning.

Mama heard me a little while ago, and she asked me what I was singing about. "About the mercy and love and goodness of God," I told her. "About how he saves us in our time of need and shelters us under his wing."

I could tell she was surprised. "Do you believe what you sing about, Abi, or do you just sing the words?"

She joined me on my bed mat and took the comb from my hand. With it she helped unravel the tangles from my hair. As she worked on a stubborn knot, tears came to my eyes.

"I want to believe, Mama," I admitted for the first time. "I like this God. He's not like our gods. There's something about him that makes me want to know him better. When the workers sing songs about him and praise him—when I sing songs about him and praise him—I feel so good and happy on the inside of me. I feel . . ." I searched for the right word so she would understand. ". . . peaceful . . . I feel peaceful."

I turned around and looked into her eyes. "Is it all right that I feel this way? I don't want you to be disappointed in me. I don't want you to be angry." The pain from the stubborn tangle was gone, but the tears remained in my eyes.

Mama pulled me to her, and I could feel her heart beating fast. I'm not sure, but I think she dabbed away the tears from her own eyes. I don't think she wanted me to see.

"It's all right, Abi. I'm curious too. If it's possible that such a loving God exists, then I want to know him as well. Understand that it's difficult for me to question the existence of what I've believed my whole life. I'm not a young girl like you. If I thought I wasted my youth on foolish paper gods, then I would consider it a terrible tragedy."

I pulled Mama's hair out of her braid, and she allowed me to comb it as she'd combed mine. We were quiet for several minutes, and I could hear Papa and the boys talking in the room next to ours. A thin blanket was all that separated us, and I wondered if they'd heard us.

"Mama?"

"Yes."

"Wouldn't it be a more terrible tragedy to waste the rest of your life believing in foolish paper gods?

She smiled at me, and then she nodded. "Yes, Abi. You're very wise. That would not just be a tragedy, that would be a sin."

Three Days Later ~ An Important Lesson

When Ruth told me that we wouldn't work in the fields for the next two days, Papa decided we'd all walk into town. The spices we'd carried from Moab were nearly used up, and we were in need of other things as well.

I'd forgotten to tell Papa that the reason we weren't working in the fields was because Israel was celebrating the Sabbath. It began at sundown yesterday and ended at sundown today. I didn't understand the meaning of the Sabbath, so I didn't pay attention to it when Ruth told me. That was my mistake.

We walked into town, but it was quiet. None of the usual men were milling about the town gate, which Papa considered very odd. The baker's shop was closed. The perfumer's shop was closed. The fuller's shop and the carpenter's shop were both closed. On each of their doors, a handmade sign hung from a nail in the door. It read, "Closed for the Sabbath." Even the usual beggars weren't begging at the town entrance.

It was a far cry from the day we first arrived in Bethlehem. That day so many men were sitting at the gate, we had to wait until we found an opening in the crowd. They were discussing the news of the day, which, of course, was us. Fortunately, none of them recognized us as we pushed past them. The women walked in and out of the shops. Children ran through the streets, kicking up the dust as they played tag and raced after their parents.

Today the only sound was that of the wooden signs banging against the shop doors. Mama moaned and decided we should pay a visit to Naomi and Ruth, since we were already in town. That's when Naomi taught us an important lesson.

We gathered on a mat on the floor of the front room. It was cramped and not very tidy. I could see that there was one other room in the back. It looked to be smaller than this one. Carmelina sat with us. Even though she's ancient, she's still full of joy. I like her.

"You must observe the Sabbath. Even foreigners are expected to desist from all work and keep the day holy," Naomi told us.

"Yes," Carmelina agreed. "You should take it seriously. A willful Sabbath breaker can be put to death."

"I'm just trying to understand," Mama told her. "Why do you observe the Sabbath?"

"Because the Lord rested on the seventh day and blessed and hallowed it." Naomi sighed. "Just get all of your work done prior to sundown on the sixth day, including your cooking, and then you have the day off to rest."

Papa agreed and said it sounded like a sensible practice. "Every man needs a day off now and then anyway," he commented.

Mama and my brothers looked at him. We were all surprised that Papa agreed so readily and didn't make a sarcastic comment. This after walking all the way to town and knowing he'd have to walk all the way back with empty arms. I think he's a changed man.

Two Months Pass

The barley season has passed, and now the end of the wheat harvest is in sight. My arms are strong and brown from the sun, and my back has lost its weakness. I remember how I complained when I went with Papa into the fields with the flocks and had to walk no more than a day! I'm sure I've walked at least two days' journey for every day I've spent in the grain fields.

Ruth and I have grown quicker at gathering

and threshing, so we collect far more grain than we used to. Recently Boaz has made a habit of appearing more often in the fields with the harvesters. Out of the corner of my eye, I see his head turn toward Ruth. Although she doesn't appear to notice, I know she's aware of his presence. She stands a little bit straighter, she talks a little bit more quietly, and her cheeks stain a delicate pink.

When he isn't present, I notice her head slowly swivel around the fields. "What are you looking for?" I've asked her many times, turning my head as well.

"Oh, nothing," she murmurs, but I can tell she's disappointed.

Last night when Mama and I prepared for bed, I asked her what she thought of Boaz. She combed out her long hair, and then she took the comb to mine. It's become a habit of ours to talk during this time.

"Well, I already know from what you've told me that he's good to his workers and sensitive to those in need," she replied. "I've also heard that he's a man of his word and very responsible. Bethlehem isn't so large, and people here, like everywhere, enjoy gossip. If the rumor is that he's a good man, then that usually means he's a good man."

Her answer satisfied me.

While Ruth and I walked to the fields, I asked her if she thought she'd get married again someday.

"I'd like to," she answered. Her voice was low and quiet. "I've always dreamed of having children."

She jabbed me gently in the ribs. "What about you, Abi? Do you think you'd like to get married one day?"

I felt my face grow hot and knew I was blushing. "I suppose so, "I told her. "But any boy I marry has to be like my father and my brothers. He has to be smart and funny and kind."

We put our arms around each other and walked close, but before we reached the field, I decided to ask her one more question. "If you were to get married again, what would you want your new husband to be like?"

Ruth put her hands on her hips and laughed. "Abi! Why all the questions about me getting married?" I smiled at her and shrugged.

"All right, then . . . Let's see . . ." She stared into the fields where Boaz was talking to one of his workers. I watched her eyes follow him as he walked, and she was quiet for several minutes. "I would like for him to be kind and generous and loving," she said after several minutes. Her eyes never left him as she spoke.

Grasshoppers in the Groves

There's a grove of olive trees not far from our camp that I've wanted to explore since we arrived. Papa said I should take Zibby with me, because foxes and jackals like to rest in the shade of the trees' wide boughs during the heat of the day.

Zibby has become a dedicated and loyal sheepdog. Even though I coaxed her from the field with a bit of cheese and she dashed ahead, eager to explore with me, she glanced over her shoulder several times as though she was pained to leave her post.

Sure enough, Papa was right. As we neared the grove, two foxes scampered away, their bushy tails bobbing as they ran. Zibby flew after them until I whistled for her to come back. She stopped and looked at me. I know she was tempted to ignore me and chase them through the hills, but she walked back with slow, deliberate steps. Her head was low, and her eyes were wet with disappointment. The foxes' scent hung in the air, and she whined for several minutes until she discovered another, more lively amusement—grasshoppers!

The grasshoppers flew out of the wild grass as she walked, and she began to prance about, jumping out of their way at first and then trying to catch them beneath her paws. I laughed until my stomach hurt. I'm even laughing now as I remember how funny she looked!

The trees are planted far apart so the sunlight can feed and ripen the fruit. I was excited when I found the patriarch of the olive trees in the middle of the grove. He was taller than the rest, and his huge, gnarled trunk was split in the middle where another tree had grown. The roots were spread wide, and his thick, knotted branches were bent low to the ground.

Papa once told me that trees like this are well over a hundred years old. I stood beneath the boughs and wondered what this ancient tree had seen, who had picked his fruit, and what children had climbed his trunk. I thought the old tree must have many stories to tell if he could talk.

The leaves of the olive trees are narrow and pointy. They're gray green on the top and silver beneath. Since it's spring, tiny buds are blooming into clusters of white flowers. Honeybees buzzed this way and that, anxious to suck out the pollen. The trees that are younger than five years don't have any flowers yet. They're still small and slender, and their bark is a smooth silver gray.

I sat beneath the old tree for a little while. There was a nest in the branch far above me, and I watched two doves fly in and out. When one returned I heard a chorus of little birds cheeping. I love spring. It's a season of new births and rebirths. Our family seems happier since we came here. Perhaps it's because we're away from people like Gershom who always made us feel bad.

I must have fallen asleep for a few minutes, cozy and content. The birds were singing cheery songs, and the leaves were rustling together in the breeze. I had't felt so peaceful in a long time. Zibby woke me up with a sloppy kiss on my nose. When I opened my eyes, she was staring at me, panting. She was thirsty, and I hadn't brought any water. I'd forgotten to bring you too, diary. It would have been a perfect place to write for a little while.

When we left we passed several olive presses. They look like large, round tables made of stone. They're used to hold the olives. On top of each one is a circular stone wheel, which is used to crush the fruit. I've noticed that wherever there's an olive grove, there's an olive press close by. I suppose it's easier to press the olives at the grove rather than haul the fruit farther away. Anyway, we'll have to wait until the fall for the fresh fruit and oil. Olives aren't harvested until then.

As soon as we started back, Zibby trotted on ahead as far as she dared without losing sight of me. I could tell she was frustrated that I didn't trot like her. When Asher saw us he whistled, and Zibby was gone in a flash.

I could smell our supper cooking before I ever reached camp. The other day I surprised Mama with a sack of freshly harvested peas and lentils, and I could smell them simmering together in a pot of thick stew.

During supper I told Papa that if he decided to stay in Israel, we should plant an orchard with several olive trees. That way we could grow our own olives. I expected him to laugh and tell me that we wouldn't be staying in Israel, but to my great surprise, he didn't. He said, "That's an excellent idea, Abi. I've always wanted an olive orchard. I'd also like a garden where I can plant chickpeas. I'd like to feast on hummus again."

The Next Day ~
Zibby Has a Friend!

I was wrong about why Zibby wanted so badly to return home yesterday. She's an excellent sheep-dog, but it seems she isn't as devoted to her sheep now as she is to her new friend! Of course, Ahmed is very disappointed about this. He told me a stray dog has been hanging around the camp for more than a month now. Zibby ignored him at first, but he worked his charms on her, and now they're inseparable!

Mama laughed when I told her. "It's spring, Abi, a season of new beginnings. Love is in the air."

Papa was just coming in, and when he heard Mama, he scooped her up in his arms and kissed her! I've never seen him like this. I guess Mama hasn't either, at least not in quite some time. She blushed until her face was the color of a tomato and shooed him away. I heard him laugh and sing all the way to the fields.

Naomi's Plan

What an incredible night it's been. It's early in the morning, and I've had little sleep. The sun is just now rising, and so are Mama and Papa and my brothers. I have to leave for town in a short while, but first I must coax Ahmed to come with me. I'm sure Mama won't let me go there by myself yet.

More of this later. First I must explain what happened last evening . . .

Ruth and I finished our work in the fields earlier than usual. All day Ruth rushed, moving faster and faster until I had to beg her to slow down. We usually threshed in the evening when the air was cool, but we gleaned our wheat early and had to thresh when the sun was hot on our backs and necks.

She was distracted as well, and when it was time to return home, she asked if it was all right if she didn't walk home with me. "It's just a short way to your camp. I know you'll be fine," she told me. "Tomorrow I promise to go with you again like always."

I pulled her into the shade for the first time all day. "I'm not a child anymore," I said. "Next month I'll be eleven years old. Will you please tell me what's wrong? I can see that you're not yourself."

Ruth stared at me for a moment. You're right," she murmured. "I owe you an apology. I've fretted all day about what I must do. I should have told you about it." She took my hand and squeezed it. "You're like my sister, after all, and you're the dearest friend I have."

She explained that she had to return to Carmelina's house right away so she could change her clothes.

"Why?" I asked her. "Where are you going?"

"To Boaz," she replied. "Naomi wants me to go to the threshing floor when Boaz has finished his supper and is resting. He sleeps there because he winnows at night when the breeze blows the strongest."

"Then I'm coming with you," I told her. "It's not safe for you to go there by yourself at night. I'll hide among the trees and wait for you. I don't know why Naomi wants you to do this, but I know she's wise, and she listens to her God."

I begged Ruth to come home with me so I could ask Mama's permission, and then we walked to Carmelina's house together.

Naomi helped Ruth wash her face and arms with scented water. She brushed her hair until it glistened before she poured several drops of perfume over her hair. Ruth took the slender alabaster bottle from her hands and held it to her nose. "Rose oil! Naomi, where did you get this?"

Naomi smiled and turned her head toward Carmelina. "It's a gift from our friend," she replied. "You'd be surprised at what this woman has hidden around this house."

Carmelina laughed, and she looked like a little girl to me. I didn't notice the wrinkles and the brown, papery skin. I saw only the mirth in her eyes and the happiness in her smile.

"When I was young, I was not so poor," she told us. "Nor was I was so frail. My bones were strong like yours, and my hair flowed down my back like a silk shawl." Her eyes became dreamy. "Some even said I was beautiful."

I felt my eyes fill up, and I went to her and touched her hand. "I think you're still beautiful," I told her.

She laughed again. "Naomi, dab some perfume on this child as well. She's as lovely as a flower, and she deserves to smell like one too."

Naomi let several drops fall onto my head, and the scent of roses hung over my head like a halo. It reminded me of the time in Moab when Ruth and I were scented with frankincense at the trade caravans.

Carmelina hobbled over to Ruth and draped a veil as large as a sheet over her head and shoulders. It was red silk, the most beautiful veil I'd ever seen. I heard Ruth catch her breath and watched her run her fingers over the soft fabric. "I can't possibly wear this," she whispered. "It's far too beautiful."

Only the finest ladies wear red silk. The poor or the common, like us, wear plain blue cotton scarves. Sometimes they're striped with white and sometimes they're made of linen, but they're never red and they're never silk.

"You deserve this and more," Carmelina continued. "It's a mere token of how the Lord will reward you for your faithfulness and your generosity. As you have given in your life, so you will be repaid."

Ruth looked lovelier than I'd ever seen her.

"It's time," Naomi said. "Remember everything I told you, and God will make a way."

To Continue . . .

It was nightfall by the time we arrived, and we hid behind several trees many cubits away from the threshing floor. We were far enough away to feel safe but close enough to watch the activity. Several of the men were still winnowing, digging their forks into the piles of wheat and tossing them into the wind. The breeze blew the chaff in our direction, and we could smell the earthy grain as it hung in the air.

Boaz appeared and walked toward the men,

and I could feel Ruth stiffen beside me. "I don't even know why Naomi sent you here," I whispered. "You haven't told me."

"Naomi told me that Boaz is a cousin to Elimelech," she explained. "Since he's kin, that could make him our kinsman-redeemer."

I shook my head. "I still don't understand what that means."

"The Israelites take care of their people, Abi. If a man dies and leaves a woman both widowed and childless, it's the responsibility of the nearest relative to take care of her. Naomi hopes that since Boaz is related to Elimelech and I'm the widow of Elimelech's son, Boaz will take it upon himself to care for me."

I touched Ruth's arm. "Do you mean marry you?"

"Yes, Abi." The moonlight was reflected in her eyes, and they glowed like little fireflies.

"Well done," we heard Boaz say, and we turned to see him pat the men on their backs. "You've put in a fine day's work. Go home to your families now. I have no one waiting for me.

I'll rest for a while, and then I'll continue the work."

"Do you see?" Ruth asked absently. "He's a good man, a good master. He takes care of those around him." I watched her follow his every move with a slight smile on her lips.

The men left, and we waited while Boaz ate his supper. My stomach was grumbling, and I watched Ruth touch her own belly. Neither of us had eaten, and I thought I'd pass out from hunger if I had to watch him put one more morsel into his mouth.

Finally he lay down at the far end of the grain pile and covered himself with his cloak. "We have to wait until he's asleep," she told me.

We sat down, and Ruth pulled me close to her, resting my head against her shoulder. The grass was soft and cool, and my eyelids were heavy. I must have fallen asleep then, because I awoke to Ruth's hand nudging me as she tried to rouse me from my dreams.

"Stay here," she said in a hushed voice. I watched her move toward Boaz, her red veil catching the breeze and floating around her like wings. She lay down at his feet and lifted up the tail of his cloak to cover herself.

I waited, leaning against the tree trunk and holding my breath until I began to feel dizzy. The bark was scratchy against my cheek, but I was too tired to care. My lids grew heavy, and once again I fell asleep.

I awakened to a voice and sat up, startled. The moon had moved in the sky, so I knew I'd been asleep for several hours.

"Who are you?" I heard Boaz whisper. Something had startled him from his sleep, and he awoke to find someone at his feet. He didn't realize it was Ruth.

I watched his head whirl around. I was sure he was looking to see if there was anyone near, anyone who might notice that a woman was with him on the threshing floor.

"I am your servant Ruth," she replied in a trembling voice. "Spread the corner of your garment over me, since you are a kinsman-redeemer."

Boaz sensed her fear, and his words were

kind and comforting. "The LORD bless you, my daughter," he replied in a calm, reassuring voice. "This kindness is greater than that which you showed earlier. You have not run after the younger men, whether rich or poor. And now, my daughter, don't be afraid. I will do for you all you ask."

I was touched by the tenderness in his voice, and I wondered if this was how it was for Mama and Papa. Did he talk to her in a loving, protective away, and did she look at him with moonbeams in her eyes when they first fell in love?

Boaz's voice brought me out of my daydreams. "All my fellow townsmen know that you are a woman of noble character. Although it is true that I am near of kin, there is a kinsman-redeemer nearer than I. Stay here for the night, and in the morning if he wants to redeem, good; let him redeem. But if he is not willing, as surely as the LORD lives I will do it. Lie here until morning."

Several more hours passed, and once again I fell asleep. Ruth didn't appear by my side again until the sun broke in the east. "Hurry," she said, "we must go before anyone recognizes us. People will assume the worst if they see us leave the threshing floor in the morning."

Her shawl was weighted down with the six measures of barley Boaz had poured into it, and she couldn't walk fast with all of the weight.

"He told me I shouldn't go back to my mother-in-law empty-handed," she said and smiled. "Send your brothers to town tomorrow, and I'll give them some to carry home."

"Wait, Ruth," I said. The coolness of the morning had awakened me, and I was remembering what had happened during the night. "Last night before you fell asleep again, Boaz talked about a kinsman-redeemer nearer than him. What does it mean?"

Ruth explained that there is a relative in town who is more closely related to her and Naomi than Boaz is. Naomi still has a piece of land that belonged to Elimelech, and whoever is the closest kinsman-redeemer has the first right to buy the property. Boaz couldn't marry Ruth and claim Elimelech's property for them without first asking the other relative if he wanted it.

Ruth doesn't know it, but I'm going to town to find out what happens. Boaz and the other relative will probably meet at the town gate where all the men gather. I just have to find one of my brothers and ask him to take me. Asher is the better choice. Ahmed will ask too many questions.

Later

Oh, I have much to tell you. I've just returned from my trip to town. I'll start where I left off so there's no confusion . . .

Papa had Asher busy with chores, so I had no choice but to ask Ahmed. It was just as I suspected. He was full of questions.

"I need you to take me into town, Ahmed."

"Why do you need to go into town?"

"There's something important I have to do."

"In town? Since when do you have important things to do in town?"

"Since this morning. Please, Ahmed. It's important. I'll explain later."

"Well, can it wait? There's a hole in the sheep pen, and I'd like to help Papa fix it."

"No! If I don't go now, it may be too late. How many times have I asked you to do things for me?" I inquired.

Ahmed studied me for a moment and then sighed. "All right, all right," he agreed. "Let's get it over with, but I want a full explanation on the way." He sounded like Mama, but I didn't dare tell him that after he had agreed to take me.

The town gate is a roofed building that has no walls. Every time we've come to Bethlehem, except the day of the Sabbath, it's been bustling with activity. Today the men were milling about in small groups, and many of the merchants had set up temporary shop. I saw Boaz right away. He was sitting at the entrance, where he had a clear view of everyone who came and went.

"There!" I told Ahmed and pointed him out. "That's Boaz. He's the owner of the fields. He'll marry Ruth if Naomi's other relative doesn't."

Boaz was looking about, but I took a chance

and moved a little bit closer. There was a small stall of fabrics, and I hid behind it and watched. A man walked by the gate, and I heard Boaz call to him, "Come over here, my friend, and sit down."

Ahmed was a few paces behind me, and I pulled him closer. "I think it's him, Ahmed! I think it's the relative."

A group of ten older men gathered around them, and Boaz asked them to sit down as well. "They must be the town elders," Ahmed told me. "Whatever Boaz plans to ask this man, he wants to have the town elders witness the conversation. I've heard of gathering two or three together but not ten. It must be a very important business matter he wants to discuss in front of them."

Boaz turned to face the younger man. "You remember Naomi?" he inquired.

The man nodded. "Of course, of course," he replied.

"Well, she's come back from Moab," Boaz replied. "She wants to sell the piece of land that belonged to our brother Elimelech. I thought I should bring the matter to your attention and suggest that you buy it in the presence of these seated here and in the presence of the elders of my people. If you will redeem it, do so. But if you will not, tell me, so I will know. For no one has the right to do it except you, and I am next in line."

At once, the younger man said, "I will redeem it."

I gasped, and one of the elders turned to look in my direction. Ahmed pulled me down behind the merchant's stall. "What's wrong with you?" he whispered.

"If he redeems the land, he has to marry Ruth!" I told him. "He can't marry her, he just can't. She's in love with Boaz, and Boaz is in love with her."

Ahmed opened his mouth to say something, but Boaz's voice interrupted him. We stood up.

"On the day you buy the land from Naomi and from Ruth the Moabitess, you acquire the dead man's widow," he told the other man. "In this way it is possible to maintain the name of the dead with his property."

I tugged on Ahmed's arm. "I don't understand. What's he saying?"

"He's telling the other man that in order to get the land, he has to marry Ruth," Ahmed said.

I held my breath. I could hear my heart pound in my ears. "Then I cannot redeem it," he announced. "You redeem it. Buy it yourself." He bent down and took off his sandal and handed it to Boaz.

I didn't have to ask Ahmed about this, because I'd seen Papa do it many times. When one man took off his sandal and handed it to the other, the deal was done.

Boaz turned to the elders and all the people. His eyes passed over the crowd, and he smiled when he spotted me beside the merchant stand with my brother. He recognized me! All this time I thought he barely noticed me and wouldn't recognize me outside the fields.

"Today," he announced to the crowd, "you are witnesses that I have bought from Naomi all the property of Elimelech, Kilion and Mahlon. I have also acquired Ruth the Moabitess, Mahlon's widow, as my wife so that his name will not disappear from among his family or from the town records. Today you are witnesses!"

One of the elders spoke out, "We are witnesses. May the LORD make the woman who is coming into your home like Rachel and Leah, who together built up the house of Israel. May you be famous in Bethlehem. May the offspring the Lord gives you by this young woman be honorable and noble!"

I ran all the way to Carmelina's house, and Ahmed didn't try to stop me. I didn't even have time to knock on the door before it opened. Ruth stood there and stared as if she'd expected me to knock on the door at that instant. I was so startled, I forgot for a moment why I'd come.

She pulled me in, and Carmelina and Naomi circled around me.

"Child, did you see Boaz?" Carmelina asked.

I nodded.

"Did you see the other relative?" Naomi inquired softly.

I nodded and looked at Ruth. She still hadn't said anything. She just stared at me and waited.

"He decided not to redeem the property," I said and burst into tears.

Ruth's face turned white, and I watched her sway to the side. Naomi grabbed her arm.

"Who, child?" Carmelina cried. "Who decided not to redeem the property?"

I realized the confusion and tried to correct myself. They thought I was crying out of sadness, but my tears were pent-up drops of joy.

"The other relative isn't redeeming the land," I reassured them. "Boaz is. He's going to marry Ruth!"

Ruth collapsed into a chair, and Naomi threw up her hands. "There is none like Jehovah," she cried. "There is none like Jehovah!"

Two Moons Later

I have very little papyrus left, so this will be my last entry in this diary. Papa promises me more paper soon. The road from Egypt passes right through Bethlehem, and the trade caravans always carry papyrus from the Nile River.

Several important things have happened since I last wrote. The most important one you can probably guess. Boaz and Ruth were married! Is that not the most exciting news in the whole world? Carmelina was right when she said the Lord would repay Ruth for her faithfulness and generosity. When Ruth and Naomi arrived in Bethlehem, they had little more than the clothes on their backs. Now Boaz's wealth belongs to them! They're wealthy and respected in town. The same women who shunned Naomi when she came to town now crave her company.

As if this isn't enough, I just found out that Ruth is carrying a child! I remember when Ruth told me that she dreamed of having children, and now Naomi will be blessed with grandchildren. I told this to Papa, and he said a beautiful thing. He said the God of the Israelites appears to be like a father to his people. He said, "It's as if he enjoys blessing them like a father rewards his children." His eyes were misty when he told me this.

I believe that's true. I don't miss Moab very much. I have fond memories of my homeland, but we're all happy here. We're getting to know this God of Naomi's, and we want to know him better. Naomi said it's too late to turn back. Once we've tasted the wonders of him, we can no longer forget him. Even if we turn our backs on him like the Israelites do sometimes, we'll always be drawn back to him, and he will always wait for us.

I asked her why this is so. "It's simple, Abi," she told me. "He is the living God. He is the breath in our nostrils, the beat of our hearts, the blood in our veins. We cannot escape the love of our creator. The love Boaz shares with Ruth, as beautiful as it is, is so small in comparison to God's love for us."

I truly believe he has sheltered us under his wing, just like Boaz said. He has taken care of us since we arrived. Papa said we'll be able to buy our own land and build our own stone house soon. He said he wants to raise his grandchildren here.

Now for another bit of exciting news: Zibby

is a mommy! Two days ago she gave birth to a litter of six pups, four boys and two little girls. Her friend, whom I've named Sheshai, has come to live with us. Ruth was the one who suggested the name. She said that in Naomi's language Sheshai means "noble," and she thought it fitting for Zibby's handsome, proud friend.

Sheshai didn't have a home, and every day he inched nearer to the camp. Zibby whined and coaxed him closer until Mama gave in and began to feed him. Now he curls up with Zibby and the pups every evening. Since we arrived in Bethlehem, we've had great increase. Instead of one dog, now we have eight! Even our flocks have multiplied. Ahmed said if they continue to multiply, we'll need every one of the pups to herd them.

I'm sitting on the hill behind our camp, watching the sun fade over the Salt Sea and bathe it in a golden light. It was an adventure traveling to Israel, and I'm glad now that Papa was bold enough to make the trip. He's taught me to be more courageous. He was devoted to the memory of his friend Elimelech by watching over his wife and daughter-in-law in much the same way Ruth was devoted to Naomi. They've all taught me what it means to be faithful.

Naomi trusted her God to take care of her even when she had nothing. She taught me that her God is deserving of our trust. I believe he led us through the wilderness and rewarded us with an oasis in Jericho. I believe he carried us up the ascent of blood to the city called Yerushalayim, where he rewarded us with peace. We knew our long journey was almost over.

He called Naomi to Bethlehem and promised her bread, but because we were faithful to follow her, we were all rewarded with bread—more bread than we can eat. Mama has said it wasn't just Naomi and Ruth who were redeemed, but all of us.

"What does it mean to be redeemed?" I asked her.

"It means that once we were held captive. You can be captive to many things—to gods that do not live, to a land that does not love, to a life that does not fit. We were prisoners in our own bodies, but the God of Abraham freed us. First he freed our hearts, and in doing so he freed our lives. He lives, Abi. This God lives."

From where I sit, I can see the plains of Moab. What was it the merchant said to Ruth and me that day? *Now the evil that has clung to your skin like a black veil will leave you. It is your lucky day.*

I don't believe it was luck though. I've made a decision. No longer will I say, "Naomi's God" or "her God" or "the God of Naomi" or even "the God of Israel." From now on I will say, "my God." He is my God, and he lives. I know he lives.

Epilogue

Seven months after Abi's last entry in her diary, Ruth gave birth to a boy. Naomi and several of the women of Bethlehem were present at the birth. When the baby was delivered, the women crowded around Naomi and exclaimed, "Praise be to the LORD, who this day has not left you without a kinsman-redeemer. May he become famous throughout Israel! He will renew your life and sustain you in your old age. For your daughter-in-law, who loves you and who is better to you than seven sons, has given him birth."

Naomi picked up her only grandchild and laid him tenderly in her lap. "Naomi has a son!" the women proclaimed, and they named him Obed.

Obed grew up and married, and his wife gave birth to a son called Jesse. When Jesse grew up and married, his wife gave birth to David, the great-grandson of Boaz and Ruth. Young David cared for his father's sheep in the fields of Bethlehem and was used by God at an early age when he fought the giant Goliath and won. He was later anointed king by the prophet Samuel and was considered the greatest king Israel has ever known. Naomi's hometown of Bethlehem came to be called the City of David.

Naomi and Ruth knew that God had restored their bushels with grain and their houses with the laughter of children. They didn't know that long after they died their inspirational story of love and devotion would be included in the Bible and retold to millions around the world.

Carmelina surprised everyone. When she died, Naomi found a note directing her to a secret cellar whose door was hidden beneath several rugs. Naomi descended the narrow steps with a clay lamp and found many bags filled with silver and gold pieces, precious stones, silks, and fine linens. Another note, found in the cellar, stated that all the treasures were to be given to Abi's family.

Naomi and Ruth were already well provided for by Boaz's wealth.

Carmelina's generosity enabled Abi's father to buy a large piece of land in Bethlehem. He built the stone house he dreamed of, and he built houses for each of his children when they married. Abi, Asher, and Ahmed helped him plant an olive orchard, vines, and a large garden, which included chickpeas. Every year thereafter Abi's mother made hummus, and they were able to enjoy their favorite Moabite meals in their new homeland.

Asher and Ahmed married women from Bethlehem and lived in the stone houses their father built. Their flocks continued to increase until they were so large that they had to hire young shepherd boys to help tend them. Eventually, Abi's family became known in Bethlehem as the wealthy Moabites who loved and served God.

Abi married too, and her children played with her brothers' children, chasing grasshoppers in their grandfather's olive orchard.

Zibby lived many happy years and gave birth

to numerous pups in her lifetime. It is said that her descendants still live in Bethlehem, herding the flocks of their masters in the rolling hills of Israel.

In Abi's later years she received word of Ruth's death. Not long after, Obed arrived at her house and pressed a small red package into her hands. Abi ran her fingers over the soft, red cloth, and when she loosened the edges, it fell open. It was the red silk veil Ruth had worn on the night she visited Boaz on the threshing floor.

When Abi held it to her cheek, she noticed that something sparkling in the corners. Four glass beads of yellow, red, blue, and green had been sewn to the edges. Abi touched the smooth glass until her fading mind was rekindled with the memories of her life in Moab. She was transported to the king's highway and the merchant caravan where the old trader had placed the glass beads in Ruth's hand as a token of his appreciation for her beauty.

In her mind she walked again with Ruth to the smaller caravan from Arabia where their hair was scented with frankincense. Abi absently lifted her gray hair to her nose. She could almost imagine that the scent of musk and lemons still clung to her hair. Suddenly she saw the face of the old merchant and heard his words as if she were listening to him now—*Now the evil that has clung to your skin like a black veil will leave you. It is your lucky day.* Her skin prickled.

This painting, by Pre-Raphaelite painter Thomas Matthews Rooke, portrays Ruth kneeling at the feet of Boaz, the wealthy landowner who was to become her husband. In her lap she holds the meager pile of grain gathered during many hours gleaning in the fields.

Scenes of sacred history were often told through the delicate, painted pictures of "illuminated manuscripts." This
one is thought to have originated in France in 1250. Here,
Ruth threshes her gleanings and brings the grain to Naomi
(Ruth 2:17–19); Naomi gives counsel to Ruth (Ruth 3:1–5);
the sleeping Boaz is joined by Ruth while his corn is being
threshed (Ruth 3:7).

On this page of the illuminated manuscript, Boaz sends Ruth
away with six measures of barley, which she brings to Naomi
(Ruth 3:14–18); Boaz consults his kinsman and the elders of
the city (Ruth 4:3–8).

In this painting by
Thomas Matthews
Rooke, the story of
Ruth unfolds. Naomi
is shown beside Ruth,
beneath a spray of
vines, tenderly cra-
dling her grandson,
Obed. He is the infant
son of Ruth and Boaz
who have since wed.

Ruth looks on, contented, while Naomi wraps her arms around a growing Obed in this 1859 oil painting by Emile Levy.

Time has passed in this last painting by Thomas Matthews Rooke. A grown Obed is portrayed as a devoted son as he holds the arm of his aging mother, Ruth, and leans close to her.

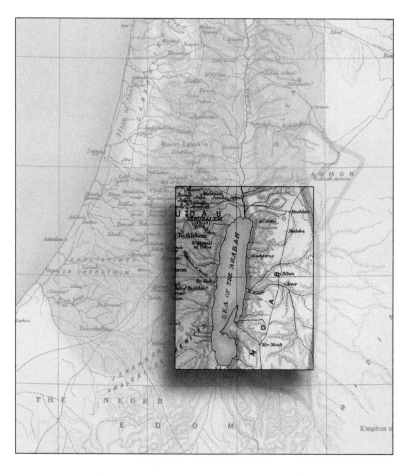

A map of ancient Palestine. A shadow box highlights the
area around the Salt Sea, also called the Sea of Arabah,
including Moab.

Abi's Home

The story begins in the village of Dibon in the land of Moab, east of the Salt Sea. It moves west to Bethlehem in Judea, in the land of Israel, and is set (approximately) in the year 1200 BC.

The People Abi Wrote of Most

Ruth: Moabite widow, daughter-in-law of Naomi

Herself: Ruth's friend and fellow harvester *

Naomi: Ruth's mother-in-law, Elimelech's wife

Papa: Abi's father *

Mama: Abi's mother *

Asher: Abi's brother *

Ahmed: Asher's twin, Abi's brother *

Boaz: Naomi's relative, Ruth's second husband

* denotes fictional characters

The People Abi Encountered

(in order of appearance)

Elimelech: Naomi's husband

Mahlon: Ruth's first husband, Naomi and Elimelech's son

Kilion: Orpah's husband, Naomi and Elimelech's son

Orpah: Kilion's wife, Naomi's daughter-in-law

Gershom: fuller in Moab *

Carmelina: poor woman who befriends Naomi and Ruth *

* denotes fictional characters

Tracing History
The Book of Ruth

It is believed that the events in the book of Ruth took place approximately one thousand years after God told Abram to leave Ur of the Chaldeans and "go to a land I will show you." However, Bible historians and scholars are unsure of exact dates. What we do know is that the story of Ruth took place in the days when the Judges ruled, sometime between 1375 and 1050 BC.

Ruth was born in the midst of Israel's dark and troubling history when "everyone did as he saw fit." In fact, scholars believe that's why the book of Ruth follows the book of Judges in the Bible—to offer peace in the middle of a troubling chapter of history.

While some historians think the book of Ruth was written by the prophet Samuel, who anointed David, others argue that it was written after Samuel's death. No one disagrees, however, that the purpose of the book of Ruth was to show how three people—Ruth, Naomi, and Boaz —remained devoted to one another and true to God even when everything around them was uncertain.

Theirs is a love story on many levels: Ruth to her mother-in-law Naomi, Naomi to her God, and Boaz to Ruth.

Who could have known that Ruth's words to Naomi would be included in marriage ceremonies today, more than three thousand years later: "But Ruth replied, 'Don't urge me to leave you or to turn back from you. Where you go I will go, and where you stay I will stay. Your people will be my people and your God my God.'"

Who could have known that Ruth would become the great-grandmother to David, one of history's most talked about kings, in history books, churches, art, and the Bible? And who could have believed that a Moabite widow would be mentioned in the book of Matthew in a record of the genealogy of Jesus Christ, the son of David, the son of Abraham:

Abraham was the father of Isaac,

Isaac the father of Jacob,

Jacob the father of Judah and his brothers,

Judah the father of Perez and Zerah, whose mother was Tamar,

Perez the father of Hezron,

Hezron the father of Ram,

Ram the father of Amminadab,

Amminadab the father of Nahshon,

Nahshon the father of Salmon,

Salmon the father of Boaz, whose mother was Rahab,

Boaz the father of Obed, whose mother was Ruth,

Obed the father of Jesse,

And **Jesse** the father of King David.

David was the father of Solomon, whose mother had been Uriah's wife.

Solomon was the father of Rehoboam,

Rehoboam the father of Abijah,

Abijah the father of Asa,

Asa the father of Jehoshaphat,

Jehoshaphat the father of Jehoram,

Jehoram the father of Uzziah,

Uzziah the father of Jotham,

Jotham the father of Ahaz,

Ahaz the father of Hezekiah,

Hezekiah the father of Manasseh,

Manasseh the father of Amon,

Amon the father of Josiah,

And **Josiah** the father of Jeconiah and his brothers at the time of the exile to Babylon.

After the exile to Babylon, **Jeconiah** was the father of Shealtiel,

Shealtiel the father of Zerubbabel,

Zerubbabel the father of Abiud,

Abiud the father of Eliakim,

Eliakim the father of Azor,

Azor the father of Zadok,

Zadok the father of Akim,

Akim the father of Eliud,

Eliud the father of Eleazar,

Eleazar the father of Matthan,

Matthan the father of Jacob,

And **Jacob** the father of Joseph, the husband of Mary, of whom was born **Jesus**, who is called Christ.

Moab's Place in History

The name Moab was first used in the Old Testament to refer to the grandson of Lot by his eldest daughter. Lot's descendants, through Moab, chose to settle in the area east of the Salt Sea. Since this land was already occupied by the Emites, "terrifying beings" so large and strong they were called giants, the Moabites had no choice but to drive them out. They were successful, and their new homeland came to be called Moab.

The Moabites' kingdom had only three fixed boundaries: the Salt Sea and the southern end of the Jordan River to the west, the Arabian Desert to the east, and the Zered River to the south. Moab's northern boundary fluctuated throughout its history. At one time Moab extended as far north as Heshbon and covered a total distance of sixty miles from north to south. Much of the time, however, it was confined by the Arnon River to the north and covered a distance of only thirty miles from one end to the other.

Moab's neighbors to the north were the Ammonites and the Amorites, and their southern neighbors were the fierce, wild Edomites. The Moabites themselves grew to be a numerous and powerful nation, and because of their ties with Abraham, they had a degree of favor with God. When the Israelites began their final advance toward the Promised Land, the Lord had a word for them:

> Do not harass the Moabites or provoke them to war, for I will not give you any part of their land. I have given Ar [a city or district of Moab] to the descendants of Lot as a possession.
>
> Deuteronomy 2:9

Moses heeded God's word and asked the Moabites' permission to pass through the territory of Moab on the king's highway, a direct route north. The Moabites refused, and the Israelites were forced to go around Edom's southern and western borders on the less convenient byway, the

Way of the Wilderness. Following the conquest of Canaan, Moab conquered Jericho and oppressed Israel for eighteen years. The oppression finally ended when Ehud, judge of Israel, killed Moab's King Eglon.

The language of the Moabites was a dialect of Hebrew, and the pagan gods they worshiped were similar to those of the Canaanites.

In 1868 an inscribed stone three feet high and two feet wide was discovered in the remains of Dibon, an important ancient city in Moab. It is known as the Moabite Stone or the Mesha Inscription, and it is the most extensive piece of carved writing ever found in biblical Palestine. Much of what we know about ancient Moab was uncovered from this stone. The writing was dated to 850 BC, and the author was Moab's own King Mesha. It can be seen today in the Louvre in Paris.

Not long after the date on this stone, Israel, Judah, and Edom united in an attack against Moab. The Moabites, pushed into the interior of their country, watched helplessly as their cities and farms were destroyed. King Mesha was shut up within the walls of Dibon, and with thousands of people watching, he killed and burned his child in an attempt to find favor with his gods. He found none.

Hundreds of years before this event, the prophet Isaiah had foretold the complete destruction of the Moabites:

> The hand of the LORD will rest on this mountain; but Moab will be trampled under him as straw is trampled down in the manure. They will spread out their hands in it, as a swimmer spreads out his hands to swim. God will bring down their pride despite the cleverness of their hands. He will bring down your high fortified walls and lay them low; he will bring them down to the ground, to the very dust.
>
> Isaiah 25:10–127

The ruins of Moab, Edom, and Ammon lay in modern-day Jordan.

Then and Now

Bethlehem, also called Ephrath, means "house of bread" in Hebrew and Aramaic. It was located five miles southwest of Jerusalem (Yerushalayim) in the hilly country of Judah, an estimated 2,550 feet above sea level. The town was on the main highway to Hebron and Egypt and was often referred to as "Bethlehem of Judea" to distinguish it from another Bethlehem farther north.

Bethlehem is famous in Bible history for many reasons. It was the burial place of Rachel, the wife of Jacob; it is said she was laid to rest "by the wayside" directly north of the city. Also, Bethlehem was home to Naomi, Boaz, and later Ruth, and was the birthplace of their great-grandson David.

David tended sheep in the lush fields famous to the city, and it was from the well in Bethlehem that three of his men brought him water when he was hiding from Saul in the cave of Adullam. He was anointed here by Samuel as king of Israel, and Bethlehem became known as the City of David.

Many years later Herod ordered the murder of all male children under the age of two years in an attempt to kill the king of the Jews. His plan failed. All of the Gospels except Mark claim Bethlehem as the birthplace of Jesus. Tradition tells us he was born in a cave close to the village, which later became known as the Grotto.

In AD 330 the emperor Constantine and his mother Helena built the Church of the Nativity over the traditional site of the Grotto. The Roman emperor Justinian later rebuilt the church in the sixth century, but much of the original church still stands. The marble alter, lined with oil lamps and incense burners, is said to lie directly over the spot where Jesus was born.

Today, Catholic and Greek Orthodox denominations share the church. The Catholic portion of the church was built over a cave where it is said the Latin scholar Jerome spent thirty years translating the Bible from Greek to Latin.

The entrance to the Greek Orthodox section of this church is called the Gate of Humility. Since its door is only three and a half feet high, all who wish to enter must be willing to crouch low. The gate and doorway were built this size by crusaders who once controlled the city in an effort to stop Muslim horsemen from using the church as a stable. The Grotto is considered neutral ground to the Greeks and the Catholics, and the priests take turns holding services there.

Modern-day Bethlehem is a village of less than ten thousand. Its hills are still ripe with almonds, olives, grapes, and figs. Throughout the years it has been a popular pilgrimage destination, with tourists flocking to both the Church of the Nativity and Rachel's tomb, as well as the fields northeast of the city. It is in those fields that the Gospel accounts say shepherds kept watch on the night Jesus was born.

Bibliography

Many sources were consulted and used in research for writing Abi and Ruth's story in the Promised Land Diaries series, including:

Adam Clarke's Commentary on the Bible, Adam Clarke, abridged by Ralph H. Earle (World Bible Publishing Co., 1996).

Atlas of the Bible: An Illustrated Guide to the Holy Land, edited by Joseph L. Gardner (Readers Digest Association, 1981).

The Bible as History, 2nd revised edition, Werner Keller, translated by William Neil; Joachim Rehork, translated by B. H Rasmussen (Bantam Books, 1982).

The Biblical Times, edited by Derek Williams (Baker, 1997).

Holman Bible Atlas, Thomas V. Brisco (Broadman & Holman Publishers, 1998).

Holman Book of Biblical Charts, Maps, and Reconstructions, edited by Marsha A. Ellis Smith (Broadman & Holman Publishers, 1993).

Jamieson, Fausset, and Brown's Commentary on the Whole Bible, Fausset, Brown, and Robert Jamieson (Zondervan Publishing House, 1999).

Lands of the Bible, J. W. McGarvey (Gospel Advocat Co., 1966).

Matthew Henry's Commentary on the Whole Bible: Complete and Unabridged in One Volume, Matthew Henry (Hendrickson Publishers, 1991).

Meredith's Book of Bible Lists, J. L. Meredith (Bethany House Publishers, 1980).

Nelson's Illustrated Encyclopedia of the Bible, edited by John Drane (Thomas Nelson, Inc., 2001).

Nelson's New Illustrated Bible Manners & Customs, Howard F. Vos (Thomas Nelson Publishers, 1999).

The New International Dictionary of the Bible, edited by J. D. Douglas and Merrill C. Tenney (Zondervan Publishing House, 1987).

The Picture Bible Dictionary, Berkeley and Alvera Mickelsen (Chariot Books, an imprint of David C. Cook Publishing Co., 1993).

Women of the Bible: A One-Year Devotional Study of Women in Scripture, Ann Spangler and Jean Syswerda (Zondervan Publishing House, 1999).

The Works of Josephus, Complete and Unabridged, new updated edition, Flavius Josephus, translated by William Whiston (Hendrickson Publishers, Inc., 1980).

About the Author

Anne Tyra Adams is the author of more than a dozen children's books, several of which have been translated into three foreign languages: Indonesian, Korean, and Afrikaans. Two of her books, *The New Kids Book of Bible Facts* and *The Baker Book of Bible Travels for Kids*, provided the foundation for writing this series, the Promised Land Diaries.

A journalist and detailed researcher, Adams is also a "student of ancient history," with a deep fascination for the Jewish culture. She used all this experience, love of history, and curiosity to write this book.

When not working on more Promised Land Diaries, Adams loves to read the classics and ancient history, taking many armchair travels in time to foreign lands. She especially loves reading biographies of famous authors.

She and her husband and their two children live in Phoenix, Arizona. They often hike in the mountainous desert surrounding their home and have been known to spot quail, coyote, an occasional fox, and many lizards. Not to be outdone by the great outdoors, they share their home with three dogs, a cat, and an assortment of little fish.

The author would like to express her deep gratitude to Caroline Jennings of the Bridgeman Art Library and Robin Stolfi and Jennifer Belt of Art Resource.

Permissions

Page 150: The Story of Ruth: Ruth and Boaz
1876–77, Thomas Matthews Rooke (1842–1942)
Tate Gallery, London
Photo Credit: Tate Gallery, London/Art Resource

Page 151: Manuscript showing Ruth gleaning
France (probably Paris), c. 1250 MS. M.63
The Pierpont Morgan Library, New York, NY, USA
Photo Credit: The Pierpont Morgan Library/Art Resource, NY

Page 152: Manuscript showing Boaz giving barley to Ruth
France (probably Paris), c. 1250 CE. Ms. M.638, f.18v.
The Pierpont Morgan Library, New York, NY, USA
Photo Credit: The Pierpont Morgan Library/Art Resource, NY

Page 153: The Story of Ruth: Ruth and Naomi
1876–77, Thomas Matthews Rooke (1842–1942)
Tate Gallery, London
Photo Credit: Tate Gallery, London/Art Resource, NY

Page 154: Ruth and Naomi
1859 (oil on canvas) by Emile Levy (1826–90)
Musee des Beaux-Arts, Rouen, France
Peter Willi/Bridgeman Art Library

Page 155: The Story of Ruth: Ruth and Obed
1876–77, Thomas Matthews Rooke (1842–1942)
Tate Gallery, London
Photo Credit: Tate Gallery, London/Art Resource, NY

Page 156: Map of ancient Palestine
Perry-Castaneda Library Map Collection
The University of Texas at Austin

Books in

Series

The author would like to thank everyone at Educational Publishing Concepts, the team at Baker Publishing Group, and Tina Novinski.

For Michal and Alexandra:
You are free to choose, but the choices you make today will determine what you will have, be, and do in the tomorrow of your life.
—*Zig Ziglar*

© 2005 by Baker Publishing Group

Published by Baker Books
a division of Baker Publishing Group
P.O. Box 6287, Grand Rapids, MI 49516-6287
www.bakerbooks.com

Printed in the United States of America

Library of Congress Cataloging-in-Publication Data is on file at the Library of Congress, Washington, D.C.

ISBN 0-8010-4527-4

Series Creator: Jerry Watkins and Educational Publishing Concepts, with Anne Tyra Adams
Cover Illustrator: Donna Diamond

The biblical account of Ruth can be found in the Bible's Old Testament book of Ruth. While these dair-ies are based on this and historical accounts, the character of Abi, her diaries, and some of the minor events described are works of fiction.